Murder in Vieux Carre and Meet Moon Boone

To Sarah
When are you coming
back to El Dorado?
Best regards,
Harmon Phillips
06/30/07

Murder in Vieux Carre and Meet Moon Boone

Norwood Phillips

Copyright © 2007 by Norwood Phillips.

ISBN: Hardcover   978-1-4257-6089-2
          Softcover   978-1-4257-6081-6

All rights reserved. No part of this book may be reproduced or transmitted in any form or by any means, electronic or mechanical, including photocopying, recording, or by any information storage and retrieval system, without permission in writing from the copyright owner.

This is a work of fiction. Names, characters, places and incidents either are the product of the author's imagination or are used fictitiously, and any resemblance to any actual persons, living or dead, events, or locales is entirely coincidental.

This book was printed in the United States of America.

To order additional copies of this book, contact:
Xlibris Corporation
1-888-795-4274
www.Xlibris.com
Orders@Xlibris.com
39391

MURDER IN VIEUX CARRE

A NOVEL

CHAPTER ONE

The studio apartment of Ace Landieux looked like a war zone. There was splattered blood everywhere. Furniture was upset, lamps broken and cushions shredded. The body lay on the floor, bathed in its own blood. There were deep lash marks over the entire upper torso and a knife had been driven from under his chin into his brain. The shoes of the policemen made sucking noises as they walked through the blood soaked carpet.

Claude Love surveyed the room. He was a tired looking forty year old, short and thin with a lock of white hair hanging down over his forehead. Wearing a wrinkled blue suit with scuffed brown shoes he surveyed the world through thick rimless glasses which gave his brown eyes an owlish look. To a casual observer he would appear to be an underpaid civil servant, which is exactly what he was. But he was not a postal clerk or a bean counter or even a dog catcher. He was chief of the Detective Division of the New Orleans Police Force. And don't be lulled into believing he was slow, because he was not. He had outsmarted some of the most devious criminal minds in the country. When they were led away in handcuffs they would shake their heads in amazement that this bookish-looking little man could have been their nemeses.

Brought up in a housing project in New Orleans, Claude learned at an early age to recognize a problem, analyze it and solve it without betraying what was going on behind those watery brown eyes.

Claude graduated first in his class at Fairmont High. Then, to the surprise of his family and neighbors, he joined the New Orleans Police Force.

Although slight in build he survived the rigorous training a recruit receives at the Police Academy. By the time he had completed his initial training his powers of perception were obvious and he was assigned to the detective division. His rise to head the division was meteoric.

Standing in the doorway of Ace's studio apartment he took off his glasses, wiped them clean and studied the bloody scene. At his side, as always, was a giant black man with a strong chin and kindly eyes. He was Alex Boudin and he was Claude's faithful friend and close associate.

"What do we know about Ace Landieux?," Claude asked Alex.

"'How do you know its Ace Landieux?," asked Alex.

"Because his name is on the mail box".

Alex's brow furrowed as he sought to place Ace Landieux. Then he spoke, "I believe he's a pimp who has a stable of three or four girls. That's all I can recall about him."

Claude asked "Who called it in?"

"The lady next door; I believe her name is Ms. Fox," Alex replied.

"Is she at home?"

"I think so."

Claude left the disheveled apartment and knocked on the neighboring door. Ms. Fox answered the knock.

When the door opened Claude saw exactly what he expected to see. A small woman with bleached red hair trying to look thirty something when she was really fifty something. A cigarette dangled from her heavily rouged lips. Her one room stank of stale cigarette smoke and cheap whiskey.

"Mam'sell, I am Claude Love with the police."

"Ain't it awful," Ms. Fox commenced. "I heard noises from next door, like he was bein' beat with a whip. He screamed these God-awful screams 'till he couldn't scream no more. When he was quiet I heard the door open and close. I waited awhile and then called 911."

"Did you see who was in the room?," Claude asked.

"Good God no," Ms. Fox intoned. "If he seen me that crazy son of a bitch would had probably kilt me too. I set quiet as a mouse til I was sure he was gone."

"Why do you say 'he'," Claude asked.

Ms. Fox looked thoughtful. "Don't know," she conceded. "There's a pretty lookin' skirt that meets him now and again. It's probably the onliest reason he kept the apartment. He sure as hell don't live there."

"Can you describe her," asked Claude.

"Good lookin' broad in a stuck up sort of way. Maybe 5'8", dressy clothes, sort of skinny" answered Ms. Fox.

"Can you describe her to a police artist," Claude inquired.

"I guess so," was her thoughtful reply. Mrs Fox was grateful for the attention. "I know one thing, her initials are L. D."

"And how do you know this?," Claude asked.

"Cause I seen it on her little black bag she always carried with her. She put it down to get out her key and I sneaked a peek."

Claude dispatched Alex and Ms. Fox off to police headquarters so she could describe the mystery lady to the police sketch artist.

With an air of resignation, Claude returned to the scene of the crime to continue his investigation.

He dispatched two of his uniformed officers to interview all of the tenants. Nothing was added to the information furnished by Ms. Fox. Indeed, the various descriptions of the mystery woman were from 25 to 40 years of age with blond or red or black hair. She was between 5'2" and 6'0" in height and weighed somewhere between 100 and 180 pounds. Some described her as appearing to be a socialite and others as a high class call girl. Claude sighed deeply. It was always like this when seeking descriptions.

Claude examined the lash marks on Ace's body. He observed the hideous knife wound commencing under the chin and extending upward through the roof of the mouth and into the brain of the corpse. He scrutinized every portion of the body and carefully examined the overturned furniture. His forensic crew waited patiently while Claude inspected and reinspected everything in the small apartment. He directed the photographers where to photograph and from which angles. Finally he allowed the medics to bag the hands of the body and transport it to the morgue for an autopsy.

Another piece of puzzling information was gleaned from Claude's careful examination. Scratched on the hilt of the knife were the initials 'S.N.'. If the initials of the mystery lady were 'L. D.', as reported by Ms. Fox, how did this tie in with 'S.N.'?

Alex returned before Claude left the apartment bearing a sketch of the mystery woman as described by Ms. Fox. Claude told Alex to take fingerprints from the corpse of Ace Landieux, also the knife and the whip and almost every conceivable place in the small apartment which might bear prints. Then he spoke, more to himself than to Alex.

"This is a crime of hate. There could be no other reason for the savage beating as a prelude to death. Could it have been one of his whores?," He didn't think so because a hooker would most probably use a knife or a small pistol, "Could it have been the savage act of a parent or brother of one of his streetwalkers?," He thought not. Most families who spawn prostitutes do not give a damn where their children are or what they are doing.

"Who was the mystery woman? Would a woman savagely beat a man half-way to death and then plunge a knife through his brain? What the killer's motive? How could the assailant silently enter the apartment? Why was there no sign of forced entry?

Shaking his head sadly Claude, with Alex at his side, exited the scene of the crime.

CHAPTER TWO

Ace Landieux arrived in New Orleans on a cattle boat as a youth of nineteen, having left Wahoo, Nebraska, under a dark cloud. Ace's sweetheart, Sally Sue Neathercutt, age fifteen, announced to not only Ace, but also to her father Simon Neathercutt, that she was with child. Old Simon had thick eyebrows, a heavy beard and hard eyes. Many of the folks around Wahoo swore that he was a duplicate of Burl Ives. He owned a large part of the county, a huge ranch, a giant herd of cattle and the general store at Wahoo. He also owned grain storage silos, a grist mill and the majority of outstanding stock in the only bank in town. It was rumored that Simon and some of his ranch hands once hanged an unfortunate drifter who was caught riding a horse bearing the Crooked S brand. Simon was not a man to be taken lightly.

Fortunately for Ace, whose name at the time was Wilbur Honeycutt, Simon liked him. Ace was manager of Simon's general store and had demonstrated good work habits and a sunny disposition. Simon was unaware that Ace was skimming from the store's profits regularly.

Simon took him aside and told him, "You're a clever young man who will most likely succeed in business and life. I'm not happy about what you have done to Sally Sue. However, since she loves you, I am giving the two of you my blessings. The wedding will be tomorrow and I will pay for a two-day honeymoon to Omaha."

Ace smiled as if he liked what he heard. "Thank you, Father, I am forever in your debt," Ace answered. And this was a true statement although Simon had no idea how true it was.

That night Ace used his key to enter the general store where he helped himself to all the cash not only in the register but also in Simon's safe. He put the two best suits in the store into his canvas bag together with several shirts and ties. There was only one pair of shoes in the store that suited him. So he took off his brogans and when he left he was wearing his new shoes. Finally, from the safe he stole a gold cross encrusted with diamonds and a petite gold chain that had belonged to Simon's late wife. Ace was well aware of his fate if Simon were to catch him. However, he rationalized that he would prefer swinging on a rope than spending a lifetime with Sally Sue.

He left in the night, driving Stanley Ray Drummond's Ford pickup truck after he had hot-wired it. He drove the short distance to Omaha and proceeded to a wharf. He scouted the water crafts moored at the dock and then left the wharf. There was only one barge, but one was enough. He drove Stanley Rays' pickup truck to an all night truck stop where he left it. Ace walked some two miles back to the dock where the sole barge in sight was moored. Since the circumstances dictated a prompt departure, he stowed away on the barge which was transporting hogs in a southwesterly direction down the upper Missouri River.

Traveling only at night he stowed away on every type of boat. He imagined Simon's hot breath on his neck and the ranch hands treating him to a necktie party. He correctly deducted that Simon would not call in the law. Ace had often heard him say, "Vengeance is mine." And when those words were uttered someone always suffered.

When he finally landed at New Orleans Ace was undecided whether to proceed further down the Mississippi to the Gulf of Mexico and onward. He checked into the Monteleone Hotel to contemplate his next move. He had slightly more than $2,000 of Simon's money left, a decent wardrobe, and an overwhelming desire to succeed at any cost. The first thing he did was buy a new pair of shoes. The pair he had stolen from Simon were beyond repair.

Some people are born blind, some with missing limbs, some mute. Ace also had a birth defect. He was born without any comprehension of the difference between right and wrong, good and evil. Ace realized this at an early age and reveled in the knowledge. From grammar school forward he cheated, lied and bullied all who came into contact with him. He stole from whomsoever trusted him.

Ace was a very handsome man who stood over 6 feet and weighed a trim 180 pounds. With coal black hair, flawless skin and clear blue eyes, he had been charming the panties off young ladies since age thirteen. He departed his hometown of Omaha at age seventeen to escape the wrath of one Stan Griggs who had vowed vengence on account of his girl friend, Lucy Belle McDougald, becoming pregnant with Wilbur's child and subsequently taking her own life. He had called at the home of Wilbur's parents armed with a Navy Colt .44 pistol. When he arrived Wilbur was nowhere to be found, having exited through a rear window. Wilbur decided it was time to flee Omaha and make his mark in the world. He left not only his family but also a string of broken hearts.

Why he chose the town of Wahoo to settle in is uncertain. He found employment at Starr Livery Stable where Simon boarded his horse Lucky Strike. Ace and Simon visited each day when Simon came by the stable for his early morning ride. Simon became so impressed with the young man that he offered him a job at his general store, which Ace hastily accepted. Less than a year later Ace was the store manger and the squire of Sally Sue. It took only a few weeks after they had met that he impregnated her and not long after that until he made his retreat from Wahoo.

During his first night in New Orleans, July 16, 1988, Ace dined at Arnaud's where he consumed a dozen oysters on the half shell, a huge tenderloin steak and a large quantity of red wine. Returning to the hotel he gave the bellman a handsome tip and was rewarded shortly thereafter by a visit from a lady of the night who used the name of Tyler. Tyler had only intended to stay an hour or so but Ace was so skilled at love making that she stayed the night. In fact, after a leisurely breakfast in bed she invited him to become her "fancy man," a Cajun term for pimp. Ace considered the proposition.

"What would my take be?" Ace inquired.

"If you furnish me a place to live, food, protection and a small allowance I weel turn over all of the money I earn to you," she answered.

"And how much is that?"

"About a thousand a week," she replied.

He did some fast arithmetic in his head. If one girl can earn a thousand a week, why not have a stable working for him? Three times one is three thousand a week. Ace decided three would be a good number. At first, he had no idea how to recruit two others. Then it occurred to him. How about the same way he charmed Tyler?

"Okay," he told her, "we will find an apartment this afternoon and you can return to work tonight."

"Do not forget, cheri, you must pleasure me when I require it."

"Of course," said Ace. But he had his fingers crossed.

Ace and Tyler rented a one bedroom with a large loft apartment at the foot of Bourbon Street near Jackson Square. Ace reasoned that he would occupy the bedroom and the three bitches could share the loft.

He acquired a second girl, Arrabelle, in the same way as he recruited Tyler. The two girls moved to the loft and visited Ace's bedroom only by invitation. Ace had found his vocation and he loved it.

Selecting the third girl for his stable caused Ace no small concern. One giggled too much, another was too large and yet another was too stupid. He was still looking when there was a knock on his door at the Monteleone. Ace opened it to find the most beautiful girl he had ever seen standing there. After a brief period of negotiations Ace agreed to pay the price she asked. He later learned that the young lady's name was Lulu Desmonde.

After a very pleasant romp in the hay Ace invited Lulu to join his stable. She refused, saying "I don't do drugs and I don't have a pimp. I'm on the way to improving my lot in life." But his lovemaking had a profound effect on Lulu. All of the others, boys and men, were simply a means to an end. Ace was different. He knew how to really pleasure a girl.

He persuaded her to agree to meet him one day a week, believing that his well-accomplished lovemaking would persuade her to change her mind. Ace was wrong. Nothing he could do would make her change her mind. However, Ace came upon the most amazing revelation: for the first time in his life he was in love. He rented a small studio apartment unknown to the other girls where he and Lulu met weekly.

Ace was swimming in money. He had increased the size of his stable to four, purchased a solid gold pocket watch and a number of colorful vests that he wore daily. He smoked Havana cigars and drank single malt Scotch whiskey.

All was going very well with Ace. And it continued to go well until that faithful day he had an unexpected, unannounced visitor in his studio apartment.

CHAPTER THREE

Simon Neathercutt had employees of limited intelligence and strong backs, one of the more notable being Silas McGruder.

Silas McGruder had been employed by Sally Sue's father, Old Simon, since he was a youth of twelve. He slopped hogs, drove tractors, pitched hay and performed all of the tasks at a large ranch that required only minimal mental acuity.

Silas was born to an alcoholic father and a weak minded mother in a three room shack on the outskirts of Omaha, Nebraska. His early years were spent being beaten by his father and neglected by his mother. He repeated the second grade at Omaha elementary before he dropped out. Never again did he darken the inside of a schoolhouse.

By the time he turned twelve the beatings had become more frequent and severe. He could not turn to his mother for help for she too was a victim of her husband's wrath. On a dark and moonless night he packed his few belongings in a paper bag, hopped a freight and left Omaha forever.

For the next several weeks Silas shared various box cars with other hobos. They were constantly on the alert for the bulls employed by the railroad whose sole purpose was to molest, beat and arrest vagrants who populated the railcars without paying fares. At each stop Silas and his fellow hobos would disembark one box car, beg or steal some food, and then hop the next available train.

At a stop in Wahoo, Nebraska, Silas had left the box car in search of food. He came upon a large vegetable garden behind a well tended house in the city limits of Wahoo. Silas was digging up turnips when he was confronted by the owner of the premises.

"What in the hell are you down' in my garden," the indignant homeowner demanded to know.

"Nothin', Sir," stammered Silas.

"You young thief, I'm takin' you to the police," the old man told him.

Silas beat a hasty retreat, leaving behind the few turnips he had harvested. As fate would decree, a police car drove by as Silas was being chased down the street. He was apprehended, hand cuffed and taken to jail.

Upon his arrival at the jailhouse Silas, still handcuffed was seated in a dark room at a scarred, bare wooden table on a rickety folding chair. An older, kindly looking man in his police uniform bearing captain's bars, came into the room and set next to Silas, whose knees were quivering so hard he could scarcely keep them for knocking together. In a soft and gentle voice the captain told him, "We don't put up with thieves in Wahoo. You little son of a bitch you will go to jail for a long time."

"Please, sir," begged Simon, "I didn't have no money and I waz hongry".

The captain asked, "When did you get here?"

"On the afternoon freight," Silas answered him.

A thoughtful look came upon the captain's face. "If I take you to court, Judge Daggett will throw the book at you. I'd say at least six months at the county farm. On the other hand if you will pay a five hundred dollar fine I may can get you off without jail time."

A sorrowful look crossed Silas' face. "I ain't got, five dollars let alone five hundred," he told him.

"We may can solve that problem," the captain told him. "I know a man who may pay your fine and allow you to pay him back by workin' on his ranch. He will retire your debt at the rate of $25.00 per month plus your room and board and $10.00 a month for spendin' money."

Silas' eyes grew round. "I'll do it."

The captain called Simon Neathercutt who came to the jail and met with prisoner and captor. A deal was struck. Unknown to Silas the "fine" was only two hundred dollars, although he was told it was five hundred. The other three hundred dollars did not find its way into the county coffers but was diverted to the captain's private stash.

Simon drove Silas to the ranch. At first glance Silas' breath was taken away. Never before had he seen such beauty. The low rolling hills were carefully groomed to give the place the appearance of a well tended golf course. However, unlike a golf course the green hills were populated with hundreds of white face cattle. A brook crossed the property and along its route supplied at least four rather large, bright blue ponds. White geese glided across the ponds. A huge red barn complimented the two story white dwelling house.

He was shown to the bunk house which was a large barren room with rows of three bunk beds on each side of the room. An iron pot bellied stove provided heat in the winter and open windows provided cooling in the summer.

"We go to work at six for six days a week and quit when it gets dark," Simon told him. "Sundays you get half a day off. I expect a full day's work."

"Yes, sir," replied Silas.

CHAPTER FOUR

The last time anyone around Omaha saw Stan Griggs was about two months before the body of Ace was found in New Orleans.

Stan had been the epitome of what an idealistic Midwestern youth should aspire to be. He was of medium height, but he had a muscular body and a boyish smile that captivated both young and old. He was fullback on the football team, captain of the wrestling team and a member of the National Honor Society.

As a young teenager he gave his heart to Lucy Belle McDougald, the homecoming queen, captain of the cheerleading team and devoted disciple to the arts and literature. She was as pretty as Stan was handsome. They made a perfect couple and each was elected as most likely to succeed. Then, during their junior year in high school Wilbert Hunnicut appeared. He stole her heart as well as her virginity.

When she learned she was pregnant she confided tearily to Stan her misfortune.

Stan told her, "I love you more than life itself. Forget about Wilbert. I will marry you and we will raise the child as our own.:

"No, my darling," she told him. "I could not love you so much had I not loved honor more. I'll not ask you to raise another man's child".

But Stan was insistent. Finally she reluctantly agreed to become his wife. Stan's joy knew no bounds. That is, until the following morning when he learned that she had taken her own life by jumping from the bridge over William Jennings Bryant creek.

Unable to avenge the death of Lucy Belle because of Wilbert's hurried retreat from Omaha, Stan Griggs' life became a living hell. He became well known at the local bars. Late at night he would haunt the empty streets. During the day light hours he searched for clues of Wilbur's whereabouts without success. His one goal in life was to locate the elusive Wilbur and strangle the life out of him.

Then one night at Moe's Bar, seated at a bar stool hunched over a glass of Sweet Lucy wine, Stan engaged in hushed conversation with a bearded man who had a large knife scar on his right cheek. The scar showed white against the black beard. To the barkeep's recollection no one at his bar had seen him before or after.

Stan handed the bearded man a legal looking document which appeared to be a deed. The bearded man left and Stan confided to the barkeep, "I'm leaving this town and no one will ever see me again". It was a true statement. He did leave Omaha and was never seen there again.

CHAPTER FIVE

Everyone knew him, or one like him, while growing up. He had a glib tongue, a happy smile and the ability to convince you to trade your favorite taw for an ordinary marble.

Samuel "Tad" McJunkin was brought up on the wrong side of the tracks in Slidell, Louisiana. He had no father and an alcoholic mother. Nonetheless, even as a small child people around him recognized that one day he would cross to the other side of those tracks and make his mark on the world. He started trading feathers from birds he would track down in the marsh and pluck at age five. He graduated upward to food stamps for moonshine. When he was at the tender age of seven, a dissatisfied customer to whom he had traded a radio that would not work for two worn tires, told him: "You're no more than a tadpole but you're smarter than a fox." The name was shortened to "Tad" and forever thereafter he was known simply as 'Tad'.

Well, he did cross to the other side of the tracks and make his mark. However, it was not the kind of mark that necessarily endeared him to others. He moved across the bay to New Orleans when he was sixteen, lied about his age so as to obtain a chauffeur's license, and became a taxi driver. Soon he learned all the ropes regarding bootleg whiskey, hookers and gambling. If you wanted something, Tad could get it for you. Whether it be a pistol with its serial number filed off, or a snort of coke or even a roll in the hay with a good-natured hooker, Tad was your man.

His old granddad cooked the moonshine for Tad's business in that area of the parish known as 'Possum Kingdom'. Too lazy to grow corn, the old man purchased it from neighbors who, when asked about their corn crop, would say, "Hereabouts, we get 'round about a hundred gallons to the acre."

Soon Tad owned the taxi franchise for Yellow Cab in New Orleans. He surrounded himself with drivers who followed his lead in furnishing sought after items and services. His fortune grew.

His real love, however, was his floating crap game. His partner in his gambling business was a one eyed hustler known as Bones LaDeux. It was rumored that Bones was caught throwing loaded dice to Carlos Mazzio who promptly relieved him of his left eye. Bones' remaining eye was a watery blue that was perpetually bloodshot from sampling too much of Tad's white lightning. Bones' particular talent was holding four dice in his left hand and throwing you any two that he chose. A dealer such as Bones was essential to a successful bust-out crap game.

One evening Bones had been busting out every anyone unfortunate enough to roll the cubes. First, he would throw regular dice at the shooter. After a point was made, Bones would toss him a pair weighted to come up with a seven every time. One evening after he recovered from his encounter with Carlos, things had been going particularly well when Bones threw the dice back to a gambler. However, instead of two dice, it was three. There was a long moment of stunned silence before Tad intoned, "Shoot, shooter, your point is eighteen."

In addition to his taxi business Tad acquired two ancient motels which were complete with hot and cold running girls, a barber shop which boasted a high stakes poker game in the rear room, and a photography studio that specialized in pornographic materials. Had Tad's dad not run away when Tad was a babe in arms he would have been proud of him.

Tad wore a large diamond ring on his pinkie finger and a diamond tie clasp. Diamond studs glistened from his French cuffs. Scores shirts of varied colors all monogrammed and a dozen tailored suits completed his wardrobe.

He lived in a stately mansion in the Garden District, dined at Arnaud's and Nola and was a regular at the Fair Grounds during every racing season. Life had been good to Tad. That is, until Lulu Desmonde entered into his life.

CHAPTER SIX

It was deep in the swamps of south Louisiana where Lulu Desmond, nee Marie Radley, was born. Her home was a four-room shack balanced perilously over green, slimy water six feet below which she shared not only with her father and mother but also six siblings, four boys and two girls. Her father was a fisherman and trapper, and the family lived largely off the fruits of his gill nets and dead falls. In the evenings he would sit by a fire with his Cajun friends and sip moonshine whiskey guaranteed to be at least six weeks old from a clear glass mason jar. Known to his trapper friends as "Boo," he was one of those rare Yankees accepted by the Cajun culture.

Boo was born in Lizzie Borden's hometown, Fall River, Massachusetts. As a young boy he aspired to be a southerner. He was a quite and reserved young man with no close friends. His father abandoned Boo, his mother, and his younger brother when Boo was twelve. As a youth of 13, he quit school and became employed at a deck hand on a fishing boat. He read all he could about the south and finally decided to migrate to Louisiana. At age 17 he ran away from home with his meager savings carrying his few belongings in a canvas knapsack. It took him more than three years to reach New Orleans.

Boo hopped a freight train and traveled across New York state into Pennsylvania where he found work at a steel mill in Pittsburgh. It was there he discovered the joys of strong drink and began to spend his spare time in the neighborhood bars which were abundant around the mills in Pittsburgh. He made no friends, only acquaintances. After nearly a year of saving that part of his money not spent in saloons, he bought a train ticket to Charleston, West Virginia, which was as far south as his small savings could take him.

For a while he worked as a coal miner in West Virginia before continuing southwest. He hitched a ride with an oil tanker truck into

Tennessee where he was hired to be a mule skinner in the log woods. It was a job he particularly enjoyed because he had a compassion for the mules that he drove and they seemed to know it. When he hooked a mule to a chain of logs, he always tried to make it a light load. The foreman quickly observed Boo's propensity to lighten their load, and after several warnings to put more logs on a load, Boo was fired.

After having been fired from his job, he was walking along side a highway near Jackson, Tennessee where he was arrested by a huge deputy sheriff and summarily convicted of vagrancy before a justice of the peace in the back room of a grocery store. Boo was sentenced to three months of hard labor at the county penal farm.

He and three others who had been convicted because they could not show a permanent address or a job, were transported in an open wagon to the place of their incarceration. They were cuffed and their legs shackled together. When the horse drawn wagon topped a hill leading to the penal farm, Boo's heart sank. There was a long, narrow wooden building. Its whitewashed sides probably once had a hint of color. No longer. Situated next to it was a pleasant bungalow which housed the warden. The guards' quarters completed the trio of misery. The interior of the prisoners' barracks was even more foreboding that the outside. Twenty bunk beds lined each wall of the building.

Boo's left leg had been shackled to the right leg of one Willie Faye Hammond. They stood at attention as a short, pasty faced man entered the room. He wore rimless eyeglasses and had a red birthmark that covered at least half of his face. With unkept brown hair and an unshaven face, he addressed the small group of new inmates.

"My name is Roosevelt Packet," he told them in a raspy, whiskey voice. "Remember that name, because you will learn to hate it like the devil hates holy water.

"We're buildin' a new cut road through some of the swampiest land you ever set your eyes on. There are cotton mouths big as your arm and gators who'll bite your leg off.

"We work from five in the morning until six at night. After your fed your supper, you will have one hour for socializing' afore lights out."

Roosevelt surveyed the motley crew. "Any questions?"

Willie Faye raised his hand, "When do we eat?", he asked.

A guard standing beside Willie Faye stuck him such a sharp blow with a night stick in the area of his kidneys that Willie Faye fell to his knees.

"You'll eat when I tell you to eat," roared Roosevelt. "And, you maggots will learn, I don't like questions".

Since he was shackled to Willie Faye's leg, Boo fell to the floor with him. He attempted to help Willie Faye to his feet and was rewarded with an open handed slap to his head by an ever present guard.

The prisoners were herded into the guards' quarters where they were issued two white pants and shirts with black stripes on then, two pair of underwear and socks and a pair of brogans.

At 4:30 the next morning the prisoners were awakened by a shouting Roosevelt bearing a cooking spoon on a tin plate. Breakfast consisted of grits and cold cornbread. They worked in the swamps clearing tress and underbrush until noon, when they were fed fried saltmeat and more grits. After half an hour break they returned to their back breaking work until six. The prisoners were then transported back to their barracks in open wagons. Around seven o'clock they were fed supper, usually watery soup and stale bread. It was lights our at eight and God help any inmate making a sound after then.

Although Boo never had had any close friends, he felt a compassion for the puny Willie Faye and undertook to perform many of the heavier tasks assigned to the younger man. Willie Faye was a twenty two year old looking like a fifty year old. He stood 5'4" and weighed in the neighborhood of 100 pounds. He had lost most of his hair and all of his teeth. Neglected since birth, he was a veteran in the world of petty criminals.

It did not take Boo long to figure out two things: First, there would be no road built through the swamp. Rather, he surmised that when the clearing was completed, levees would be built and the rich lands would then be farmed. Second, it would be foolhardy to serve his entire sentence because as soon as an inmate was released, he would be again arrested, tried and returned to the prison farm.

He began making his plans. Boo had been a quiet prisoner who did not complain and was totally subservient to the guards. In their pea sized brains the guards deduced that Boo was not an escape risk. In fact, the guards were so enamored with Boo that he was appointed water boy.

A water boy keeps buckets full of water from a spring around a mile from the work site and passes it out to inmates from a hollowed out gourd. This was a particularly pleasant job for Boo since at the prison farm, the inmates were permitted one shower per and one shave per week, he could enjoy sponge baths daily while filling the water buckets. More importantly, he could be away from the work site for up to an hour at a time.

Boo waited until three days before his scheduled release. It was logical to presume that no one would try to escape with only three days left to serve. So, by biding his time he would not be missed for up to two hours.

Although no train tracks were in sight, Boo knew that there was a track close to the prison farm because he heard a train whistle every day around two in the afternoon. Boo did not have a watch and hence he had watched the position of the sun every day. Soon he was able to tell by the sun within a very few minutes when the train's whistle would sound.

On the third day before his scheduled release, Boo picked up his water buckets and commenced to hike to the spring. However, once he was out of sight of the guards he threw down the buckets and began a fast trot towards the railroad tracks. For a short time he was afraid that he had misjudged the distance to the tracks. Then, the right of way came into sight. He settled under a large elm tree to await his ride. Soon he was rewarded with the far away sound of the steam whistle and he arose from under the tree and walked close to the tracks.

While standing on the right of way awaiting the oncoming train he heard the far away baying of bloodhounds, Boo knew that it had been discovered that he was missing. It was his only hope that the train arrived before the hounds. And luck was with him. The train slowed down but did not stop. Boo grasped the handle of a ladder and held on for dear life. From the corner of his eye he could see the approaching posse. He held onto the ladder like it was the last loaf of bread on earth. After around half an hour of holding onto the ladder, Boo was happy to see the train stop at a water tank. He stepped down from his ladder and walked along side the train until he found an open box car door. Upon entering into the car he heard a deep raspy voice:

"What's you do'n here, Sonny?" an elderly black man asked. He had a wrinkled fact and snow white hair. He wore a faded blue shirt, blue jeans and had rimless eyeglasses.

Boo decided honesty was the best course to take. "I jus' escaped from the chain gang and I'm lookin' to get the hell out of Tennessee".

"You ain't goin' far in them duds," the black man told him.

"Got nuthin' else to wear". Boo answered.

"Name is Moses", he said. "I been on th' run my own seff afore. Let me see what I got."

Moses had a large straw suit case which he opened. Inside were a variety of clothing including green Marine pants and a faded shirt with the stripe of a private first class on it. The garments were handed to Boo with the explanation that "I done got too fat to wear 'em any more. Might as well do something useful with "em".

Boo and his new friend rode the box car to the switching yard at Memphis. Boo invited Moses to travel south with him to Louisiana, but Moses politely declined, explaining "Got a cousin here in Memphis that I gotta go see. Good luck to you, boy. Wear them clothes with a lot of pride. I had 'em since the war."

Over and over Boo thanked Moses before hopping a south bound freight. He crossed the Mississippi and was stranded at West Memphis, Arkansas. He found employment again as a deck hand on a barge which steamed up the Mississippi from West Memphis to St. Louis. Boo found life on the river very pleasant. He reduced his consumption of rye whiskey and saved his money. After he had stayed on the barge for slightly over a year the itch for the deep South returned.

Boo proceeded south through Arkansas as a paying passenger on the old Cotton Belt railroad until he reached El Dorado. He walked the remaining seventeen miles to the Louisiana state line at Junction City which is located in both Arkansas and Louisiana. When he crossed State Line Road at Junction City, he placed his knapsack on the ground and kissed the ground. It had been worth the long trip.

He caught a ride with a trucker on an eighteen wheeler all the way to New Orleans. Once Boo reached the Crescent City he learned for the first time that further south were the lands of Evangeline and Gabriel, where the brackish waters were rich with shrimp, crayfish, red snappers, crabs and almost any sea food treats as could be imagined. The back-waters of the swamps also abounded in alligators, beaver, rabbits and every kind of swamp bird and duck as ever existed.

Boo knew that he had no choice but to continue south. He caught a ride ever so often but walked most of the way on his journey to Grand Isle. When he first looked at the vast swamp east of Grand Isle, he knew he was home. He had almost three hundred dollars which he had saved from his job on the river. He found lodging in the upstairs bedroom of a shrimper for which he paid $7.00 a week. After he settled in, the first thing that he did was craft a pirogue, (pronounced "pee-row") which is a small boat constructed by digging out the center of a large log. He then used his small craft to venture deep into the swamp. When he found a suitable spot he constructed a rough one room shack on four poles pounded deep into the marshy bottom of the swamp. The final touch was the construction of a dock around his castle. Upon completion he took his belongings in a canvas bag and said goodby to the shrimper who had been his landlord for a month. He moved into the swamp where he would remain the balance of his life.

Boo felt he had come home, but the home folks did not welcome him with open arms. It took a close encounter with a huge 'gator and a race through the swamp while being chased by a wild life enforcement officer to cement Boo's alliance with his Cajun neighbors.

He was sculling his pirogue through backwater when he heard loud shouts and cries for help. Following the noises to the far end of a slough he found Louie Bordeaux holding the tail of a very hostile alligator. Louie's rifle lay several feet from him. He couldn't let go of the tail for fear the gator would bite his leg off before he could reach his firearm. Had it not been for Boo, Louie would have tired, let go of the alligator's tail and furnished the gator with a gourmet dinner.

Calm as a clam Boo picked up his 30-30 rifle that had been lying on the deck of the small boat and shot the gator squarely between its eyes. The gator thrashed as a prelude to death, striking Louie's knee causing him to fall to the ground. At that time they heard muffled purr of an outboard motor.

"Eet's zee game wordin" muttered Louie through clinched teeth, while holding his injured leg. "Geet outta ear afore he geet bof of us."

"Stay here," Boo told him. He commenced sculling his small boat at a rapid clip toward the mouth of the slough. When the game warden came into sight Boo turned away from him and commenced to scull his pirogue as rapidly as he could. With the five horsepower outboard motor on his johnboat at full throttle, the game warden would gain on the fleeing Boo and then lose whatever he had gained each time his small craft collided with a cypress knee.

Finally, convinced he could not catch the elusive Boo, the game warden cut back his throttle and commenced winding his way through the swamp toward the boat launching ramp where his truck was parked.

That night Louie, his wife and their children appeared at Boo's door, bearing fried tail of the alligator which Boo had killed, a rich gumbo made with wild rice, shrimp and oysters and a large jug of white lightning. This was the most important night in Boo's life. When he won the friendship of Louie, he likewise won the friendship of every river rat in the swamps. More importantly, though, it was the night that he met Annette, Louie's fifteen year-old, black eyed daughter.

It was love at first sight. Within a month's time Boo had married her, impregnated her and added a bedroom to his shack sitting over the swamp. Life was good. Their oldest child, Marie, now Lulu, was born less than a year later. She was a beautiful child with smoldering dark eyes and raven black hair. She was, and remained so the rest of her parents' lives, their favorite.

CHAPTER SEVEN

Mardi Gras Carnival is a time for outlandish celebrations in New Orleans. It is the season immediately before Lent when people enjoy the sensual life, including, but not limited to, eating, drinking and dancing. Mardi Gras itself is the Tuesday before Lent and hence is known as Fat Tuesday. This represents the last hurrah before plunging into rice and fish on Fridays. Until 1909, a boeuf gras—literally interpreted as "Fat Bull"—walked the streets.

Krewes are carnival organizations that organize Mardi Gras parades, hold balls and have Mardi Gras as their central purpose. The Mystick Krewe of Comus coined the word in 1857. Krewes are commanded by a "Captain" and they build and store their floats for parades in secret places called "Dens."

Because of his high standing on the economic ladder, Tad was selected as captain of his krewe, known as the Mystick Order of the Eclate. They built a monster float in their Den which was a replica of a large paddle wheeler, complete with a smokestack that bellowed smoke and a paddle wheel which actually turned. On the deck there was a four piece jazz band.

A Mardi Gras Ball is unique. It is a masked dance and party hosted by a krewe to celebrate Mardi Gras. Those who are invited receive a hand-written invitation in flowing script to gain admittance to the ball. Such invitations are coveted by all but received by only a few. The Ball of the Mystick Order of the Eclate was the envy of all of the other Balls. It boasted of having a full orchestra, entertainers from Broadway and sufficient food and drink to sustain the entire French Quarter for a month. Of course, the huge King Cake is always present with its purple, green and gold colors. It has a small plastic baby inside. According to tradition, whomever received the slice of cake containing the baby will be blessed with good luck until the next Mardi Gras.

The Krewe of the Mystick Order of the Eclate consisted of an even balance of socialites, politicians and businessman. Tad, as the proud Captain of the Krewe, reigned happily over his kingdom. Life had been good to him.

CHAPTER EIGHT

Lulu hated life in the swamp. Their shack had no bathroom and consequently Lulu was forced to bathe in the bayou and wash her hair with rainwater. Except for small essentials such as salt and coffee the family lived off the land. She had not tasted sweets until age eight when she accompanied her father to Frenchy's Boat Camp at the edge of the swamp where Boo bought her five cents worth of rock candy. By the time she was ten she was making the trip alone from the Radley shack to Frenchy's to purchase coffee, salt, cornmeal and flour. Although Boo's cash supply was limited to such meager amounts received for animal pelts and alligator skins, he always had a nickel for her to indulge her sweet tooth.

It was at the boat camp where Lulu became awakened to the difference between boys and girls. She tempted the boys with coy looks and lewd promises, as a result of which she always left Frenchy's with a large sack of candies that she shared with her siblings. At age twelve she surrendered her virginity to Maurice DuBois, a young dandy who owned his own pirogue, in back of Frenchy's grocery store-bait shop. This event taught her two important things. First, sex was a pleasant experience. Second, and much more valuable, it taught her that she held an incredible power over the males of the species. From that day until she left the swamp at age sixteen she would leave Frenchy's with a large sack containing not only candy but also toilet water, face powder and even lipstick. She always left in her wake a group of satisfied, but broke, young men.

When she decided to leave the swamp her father took her in their pirogue to Frenchy's. With tears in his eyes, Boo held her in his arms

"Godspeed, my angel," he told her. "Never forget your mama and papa who love you very dearly."

Lulu told him, "When I have made my fortune I will send for you."

"No," he replied, "We will never leave. Mon cheri, we will pray that God lets us see you again."

She walked from there to a bus stop three miles away where she caught a bus to New Orleans.

When she arrived she had almost twenty dollars, of which her father had given her ten and the rest she had saved from his amorous adventures with the swamp boys. In addition, she had a small cardboard suitcase containing clean underwear and an extra blouse.

She went to a small rooming house, paid fifteen dollars for one week's rent and retired to her room. After dark, she walked the streets in the French Quarter where she earned enough money to buy some new clothes and enjoy a decent meal at a small café known as "Emil's." It became her favorite place in New Orleans.

From her first day Lulu loved the French Quarter. She would haunt the jazz bars and bistros. She spent long hours at the French Market, the Café Dumonde, and on the levee watching the cruise ships and river boats come and go up and down the Mississippi. She was content.

Little by little Lulu became acquainted with bellmen at expensive hotels in Vieux Carre. It was through them that she made the transition from streetwalker to call girl.

Lulu found a job as a saleslady at an upscale fashion shop. She divided her time between her duties as a saleslady in the day and as a call girl at night. She studied the attire of all the customers of the small but exclusive shop. At first she spoke very little but listened intently to the slow, but refined speech of their clientele. She was a quick learner. Within a year you would have mistaken her for a debutante. She had lost most of her Cajun accent and her wardrobe was impeccable.

Blanche LaGrone was the owner of the shop where Lulu worked. As she inherited the business from her mother, she had been associated with the garment industry for the better part of her life. It became apparent that Lulu acquired a knowledge of fashion second only to Blanche. It was inevitable that Lulu and Blanche were drawn to one another. Blanche believed her to be a girl with high morals, who despite her poor upbringing had overcome her meager start in life. Had someone told Blanche that Lulu made calls at night to the more expensive hotels in New Orleans she would have called him a vicious liar.

Blanche and her husband Paul had had a happy life before his untimely death several years before Lulu arrived on the scene. Her one regret was not having had children. Somehow Lulu became a substitute daughter for the one she never had. At Blanche's insistence, Lulu moved into her home which was also in the Garden District. While attending to Blanche, she continued to work as a call girl late at night. Lulu became the manager of the boutique, and it flourished under her guidance. She was the perfect substitute daughter to Blanche whose health had begun to decline.

When Blanche's condition grew critical she refused to be hospitalized. Lulu was her only attendant and was holding her hand when she died.

To the surprise of no one Blanche's will, after making a generous bequest to the Catholic Church, left the balance of her entire estate, including her boutique, her home, her money, and all of her jewelry and other personal property to Lulu. Six years after leaving the swamps of south Louisiana, Lulu was a wealthy woman.

Life had also been good to Lulu. From swamp rat to streetwalker to the upper strata of New Orleans society put her in the same class as the former street grifter, pimp and big-time gambler, Tad. As fate would have it, Lulu and Tad were neighbors in the Garden District of New Orleans although they never formerly met until the Ball of the Mystick Order of the Eclate. This does not mean Tad was unaware of his raven-haired neighbor. To the contrary, he had watched her with lustful eyes since her arrival in the neighborhood. At first he looked upon her only as a loyal and devoted servant of Madam LaGrone. However after the death of Madame LaGrone he made it his business to learn the extent of her fortune. And when he learned the true value of her estate he looked upon her with a new found respect and admiration. This woman was, indeed, worthy of his attention and his attention she got. The nature of his business dictated that he have a small army of informers and investigators. Through them he learned of Marie Radley, swamp rat and former streetwalker. It made him admire her even more.

Tad formulated a plan to meet and woo the fair Lulu. To set the plan in motion he personally saw to it that Lulu was invited to the Ball of the Krewe of the Mystick Order of the Eclate. He instructed the planner of the Ball to seat Lulu next to him.

The Ball was as festive as ever. Seated next to each other, neither Tad nor Lulu would acknowledge they knew anything about one another. However, since they were both attractive young people they were immediately drawn to one another. They danced the night away. At 5 a.m., they left for the home of J. Murry LaDeaux to enjoy a gourmet breakfast of Eggs Benedict, rare roast tenderloin of beef sliced paper thin, oysters on the half shell, Shrimp Arnaud's, and all manner of other culinary delights, washed down with aged wines and icy cold champagne. It was after 9 a.m. when the breakfast guests departed. Tad and Lulu agreed to meet again.

CHAPTER NINE

J. Murry LaDeaux was a neighbor of both Lulu and Tad, living in an old antebellum home directly across the street from both of them. Unlike his neighbors Lulu and Tad, J. Murry had been born into a great fortune.

In his early boyhood J. Murry had been expelled from some of the finest prep schools in the south. After finally obtaining his high school diploma from a small private school in New Orleans, he enrolled at Loyola where he was promptly expelled on account of running wearing only a slouch cap and a smile across the campus to win a $100 bet.

Following his exit from Tulane, J. Murry enrolled in Harvard. Life on the east coast did not satisfy him and he returned to New Orleans. Shortly after his return an event occurred that totally changed his direction in life. He and two of his friends had been haunting the bars of Bourbon Street when they were approached by a prostitute. They took her to a hotel room and after the three of them had finished with her they took turns slapping and hitting her while drinking sour mash whiskey. The three then returned to their favorite bar on Bourbon Street and continued their party. The whore, who paid protection money, swore out a warrant for their arrest. J. Murry and his fellow revelers were handcuffed and hauled to the local police station. While they were in a holding cell a short dapper man with a pencil of a mustache arrived and quietly drew the booking sergeant aside and had a whispered conversation. J. Murry, et al, were promptly released. The little man's name was Paul LaFitte, like the pirate, Jon. It crossed J. Murray's mind that Paul must have been a direct descendent of the famous pirate.

J. Murray learned the whore had withdrawn her complaint and that prompted their speedy release. Completely impressed, J. Murray asked LaFitte the secret of his success. His answer was a model of brevity: "Mi ami, wheen you have pleenty of cash, do not concern yourself with zee

37

law." J. Murray learned a powerful message that day, so powerful that it induced him to return to his studies. He completed undergraduate studies at Loyola and then was an honor graduate in law from Tulane. Regardless of all the knowledge he acquired at the various universities, that one sentence from Paul LaFitte shaped his life and his law practice forever, or at least until that faithful night at Police Plaza that he shared with Tad and Lulu.

J. Murray was indiscriminate as to his cash flow. He freely passed out bribes to police officers, to sheriff's deputies and even to judges. As a result he soon became known as the mobsters' best friend. Although born rich, he became even richer.

CHAPTER TEN

One of Tad's most successful ventures was his all-night poker game. It was played every Tuesday night in a back room of a barber shop he owned. Although Bones LaDeux was far more adept at manipulating dice, nonetheless he was always present at the big game, his one eye ever alert for card sharks and cheats. The game was table stakes with a minimum sit down of $10,000. They only played five card stud, nothing wild. It was a house rule that the game broke up at two a.m. Tad himself always participated as a player and almost always took home a large percentage of the pots.

Although Tad was an accomplished poker player he did not depend on his skills alone. He had a silver cigarette case that he used as a shiner. He placed it on the table at what appeared to be a careless angle. However, it was so placed that when he dealt he could see the hole cards of his adversaries. He only used the shiner when he dealt. The rest of the time he relied on his own skills.

J. Murray, himself an avid gambler, was not an infrequent participant in Tad's game of chance. He was a real threat because he didn't give a damn. It mattered not the size of the bet, J. Murray would call, or even raise. He and Tad, being kindred spirits, bonded. And this is the reason that he answered a late night call from Tad, dressed and journeyed promptly to Police Plaza where he found Lulu and Tad at the desk of the booking offices. It was 3:30 in the morning scarcely an hour and one half hours after the poker game had broken up.

"What in the hell are you and she doing here at this time of night," J. Murray demanded to know.

"Because she has been charged with murder," was Tad's simple reply.

CHAPTER ELEVEN

Since the grand ball and gourmet breakfast at J. Muarry's, Tad and Lulu had been seeing each other frequently. Tad did not know of Ace and likewise Ace did not know of Tad.

They became the talk of New Orleans, the handsome young people with perfect manners who dressed impeccably. They appeared at grand balls with Lulu wearing the latest creation from Paris and Tad in tails and a top hat. She wore tailored jeans with a halter top for their frequent trips through the bayous in Tad's launch. Almost weekly their photographs graced the society pages of the *New Orleans Times-Picayune*. Socialites speculated behind open fans as to when a wedding date would be announced. Since Ace did not read the society pages and was unaware of the gossip of the elite he had no idea of the relationship between Lulu and Tad. Since Lulu did not want Tad to know of Ace and their weekly meetings, she was always careful not to mention his existence to Tad. Likewise, Tad did not mention to Lulu the source of his wealth or the businesses, legal and illegal, that he controlled. However, Lulu being street-smart herself, knew all about Tad. They were a perfect couple; that is, if one considers lies and misrepresentations to be the cornerstone of a happy relationship.

CHAPTER TWELVE

Claude showed the police artist's sketch to all the tenants in the building where Ace was murdered. Those who recalled the mystery woman at all, mostly the younger men, agreed that the sketch presented a reasonable likeness of her.

It was very difficult for Claude to comprehend how a woman could have committed so violent a crime. What kind of woman was she? The one common word used by the tenants in describing her by the tenants was "cultured." How could such a woman have done this monstrous thing? But there were no other clues. He had no choice but to continue to look for the mystery woman.

Claude entered into his small office at Police Plaza. The best word to describe the office was "dark." A single overhead light bulb offered little light, even when it was turned on. And Claude did not turn it on when he was lost in thought. The walls were covered with dark paneling. The battered desk and wobbly desk chair were dark brown, and the floor was covered with a worn carpet of indeterminate color, but dark nonetheless.

Claude sat in his dark chair in his dark office and thought dark thoughts. Why had Ace been murdered? He was not known as a gambler so the murder on account of a gambling debt was highly unlikely. Besides, Ace had plenty of money and surely would have paid off a debt rather than risk dying. Could it have been revenge by one of his whores? Claude did not think so. On the streets Ace was known as a compassionate pimp who hardly ever beat one of his girls. If one of them would want to kill him she most assuredly would have used a pistol, not a blade and a bull whip. It certainly was not a case of robbery because nothing could have been gained by the robber by torturing him; and, moreover, there was a substantial amount of money is Ace's wallet.

So Claude deduced it was either the mystery woman or some one seeking revenge for Ace's past transgressions. Claude furrowed his brow. Insofar as the New Orleans Police Department had been able to determine, Ace had not come into existence until some ten years before when he broke into the business of the red light district. Since he had never been fingerprinted when he was Wilbur Honeycutt in Wahoo, Nebraska, the only prints on file identified him as Ace Landeuix. What was his past life like, Claude wondered. Did someone hate him so intensely as to beat him within an inch of his life and then penetrate his brain with a long knife? If so, why? Was the mystery woman a spurned lover who exacted revenge in such a violent way? Claude really didn't think so. No, his logical mind told him Ace was murdered on account of past sins. Another troubling matter were two small initials, S.N., scratched on the upper part if the knife. If Ms. Fox had correctly identified the initials on the overnight bag of the mystery woman as L. D., where did she get S.N.'s knife? However, as a realist he deduced that he must first identify and locate the lady woman of mystery as the initial step in solving the case.

Adding greatly to his frustration was the fact that none of the prints, other than Ace Landeuix's, found in the apartment matched any on file with the New Orleans Police Department or in the master file of the F.B.I. There were prints on the handle of the whip, but whose? So Claude formulated a plan that would lead him through the red light district of Vieux Carre to the heart of the upscale Garden District.

He dispatched his officers to canvas all areas of the French Quarter in hopes of learning something about the mystery woman. Claude himself undertook to follow through behind his cops by interviewing hookers, pimps and grifters. They all knew Claude and liked and respected him. Claude did not hassle them. He did not arrest them for following their chosen trade. Therefore, many would talk to him and to no one else, secure in the knowledge that Claude would under no circumstance identify his sources. And this is the reason that Louise Bordeaux opened up to him.

Several of the working girls had a vague recollection of a hooker whose likeness appeared on the police artist's sketch could have been one of the sisterhood. However, none knew her name. They did not believe she had a pimp. All recalled that she had left the streets years before.

But Louise related to Claude that she believed she saw the dark-haired beauty working in a boutique while she was still active in the trade at night. Louise couldn't recall the name of the store but remembered its location.

Together they went to Boutique d'Orleans. The display windows revealed very beautiful and very expensive merchandise. From French perfumes to soft nighties, the exclusive shop had it all. Mardi Gras costumes hung next to Italian shoes. Feathered fans and purple masks were there, as were designer gowns and peekaboo nightgowns. It was definitely a shop for those who were both rich and knowledgeable in the fashion world.

Together Louise and Claude entered the shop. With Claude in a wrinkled brown suit and shirt with the points of his collars turning up and Louise looking every inch a street-walker, they looked as out of place as a hot dog at a steak dinner.

Claude approached a saleslady who eyed him with scornful detachment. Claude spoke first. "Allow me to introduce myself. I am Claude Love, chief of the New Orleans Detective Bureau. I am here to speak with this young lady who works here." Claude handed her the sketch.

The sales lady, who had never before even seen a detective, let alone spoken to one, took the sketch from Claude. She pursed her lips and studied it carefully. "She does not resemble anyone who is employed here," she said. "However, she greatly favors the owner of this Boutique, Lulu Desmonde."

"May I speak with her?" asked Claude, always the gentleman.

"I'll see," was her reply as she left and proceeded to the back of the shop.

A few minutes later Lulu emerged from her office. Her gait could be mistaken for a queen, her posture haughty and her hair perfectly arranged to the last detail. Her cheeks were slightly rouged and her lipstick so pale that Claude was uncertain as to whether it existed or not. Her dress was impeccable. A large diamond supported by a heavy gold chain dangled between her ample breasts.

"Inspector Love," she said with a smile. "I am Lulu Desmonde. What may I do for you?"

"L. D., Lulu Desmonde," thought Claude as he struggled to regain his composure in the presence of so grand a lady.

"Mam'sell, regrettably there are some questions we must ask. Would you prefer to go to your office or to Police Plaza?"

The smile left her lips. "What sort of questions?", she asked, her voice growing hard.

"We understand you are an acquaintance of Ace Landeuix. Is this true?" responded Claude.

"Let us go to my office," said Lulu.

Claude nodded for Louise to leave and followed Lulu to the rear of the shop into her office. And what an office it was! It had either been arranged by a professional interior decorator or by an extremely gifted amateur. Cream-colored wallpaper with tiny red roses scattered throughout it accented the two silk tastefully arranged upholstered overstuff chairs. The large desk was snow white with a gold inlay pattern. A gold-framed vanity mirror was located behind the desk.

"Who wants to know whether I know this Ace person?" she asked.

"He was brutally murdered." Claude minced no words. "You have been identified as a person entering and leaving his apartment on Rue Bienville. Is this true?"

She took a long sober look at Claude. "What do you want of me?" Lulu asked.

"Will you submit to being fingerprinted and will you appear in a police lineup?" he asked.

"Am I under arrest?" she asked.

"No, not now," answered Claude.

"Then the answer is 'no'," she told him. "Please leave the premises."

"Oui, Mam'sell," Claude replied, bowing slightly. "I will be back, you know."

As soon as he departed Lulu put her head on her desk and wept quietly. She did not leave her office until after all of her employees had gone.

After locking the door of her shop she turned and what she saw made her blood run cold. Seated in a battered Ford coupe across the street were Claude and Ms. Fox. She recognized Ms. Fox as being Ace's next door neighbor. Ms. Fox was nodding her head vigorously.

She hurried home and called Tad at his poker game. She knew the police would be coming. Tad excused himself from the game and hurried to Lulu's home.

And right she was. Exactly one hour after she had emerged from her shop at ten o'clock, Claude and two uniformed policemen arrived at her door.

"Mam'sell Desmonde", said Claude, "You are under arrest for the murder of one Ace Landeuix. Anything you say can and will be used against you in a court of law. You have the right to an attorney. If you cannot afford an attorney, one will be appointed for you. Do you understand this warning?"

"Yes, I understand." she answered.

"Then we will proceed to the station house," he told her.

"Tad," she told him, "call Murry and have him meet us at wherever they are taking me."

She held out her wrists to Claude. "Cuffs are not necessary," he told her. "Please accompany me to the police van parked at your curb."

With Lulu leading the way, she, Claude and the two uniformed policemen walked single file with a singular purpose to the waiting van.

When J. Murry arrived at Police Plaza, Lulu was walking back into the ante-room, after having been booked, photographed and fingerprinted. She was wiping the ink from her fingertips when she entered the room. As always, male heads turned toward her.

"Murry, what can I do?" she asked. "I did not kill the man. I don't know who did it."

"Have you made a statement?" he asked her.

She shook her head.

Good," said J. Murray. "I'll arrange for a bond hearing tomorrow. Say nothing to anyone."

"You mean I must spend the night here?," she asked.

"Yes. But I will see to it that the case is assigned to a friendly judge. We should have you out on bail tomorrow," J. Murry told her.

While sitting in the ante-room she watched J. Murry work the room, slapping policemen on their backs and palming their hands with small brown envelopes. Then she noticed, of all of the cops in Police Plaza only Claude did not participate in J. Murry's charade.

"Oh, my God," she thought, "an honest cop." Being a life long resident of Louisiana, to Lulu politicians and corruption were one and the same. And an honest cop scared the bejesus out of her.

Lulu did not sleep well, but the cold, dank cell was no worse than the house of her youth deep in the bayous of South Louisiana.

The next morning she bathed as well as could be expected with only a sink and no hot water. She carefully brushed her hair and dressed in the same garments she had worn the night before. Lulu thanked her lucky stars that J. Murry had arranged for her to be incarcerated by herself.

Around 11 o'clock the jailer escorted her to a holding cell where she awaited docket call. It was after one o'clock when she and J. Murry stood before the Honorable Judge Royal X. Peabody. The bailiff intoned "State vs. Lulu Desmonde, charged with second-degree murder."

J. Murry whispered to her, "Say nothing other than 'not guilty'." If she heard him she gave no sign. She merely clenched her teeth and stood mute before the Bench. Murry and Judge Peabody exchanged slight nods.

"How does the prisoner plead?" asked Judge Peabody.

"Not guilty," Lulu said in so low a voice it was difficult to hear her.

"Speak louder," commanded Judge Peabody.

"Not guilty, your Honor," Lulu answered in a voice up a couple of decibels louder.

"Bail recommendations, Mr. District Attorney?" asked the Judge.

Young Willie Wharton was already on his feet. "Judge Peabody," he said earnestly, "this is a particularly heinous crime. The victim was savagely beaten with a bull whip before a knife blade was driven into his brain. The knife was still in the apartment and it bears the fingerprints of the defendant. She has been identified by neighbors as a frequent visitor to the deceased's apartment. The State asks that she be remanded without bail."

"Mr. LaDeaux," Judge Peabody called upon J. Murry.

"Your Honor," began J. Murry smoothly, "Ms. Desmonde is a pillar of New Orleans society. She gives quite freely of her time and money to worthy causes. She owns a very successful business. She is not guilty of this crime and is anxious to proceed with trial so as to clear her good name. She is not a flight risk and respectfully requests the Court to release her R.O.R."

"Very well," said the Judge. To Lulu he said "I am releasing you on your own recognizance. You are not to leave the jurisdiction of this Court."

"But your Honor," sputtered young Willie, "the State objects."

"Next case," said Judge Peabody.

J. Murry took Tad and Lulu to the Court of Two Sisters. Being in a particularly festive mood, he ordered champagne.

After the champagne had arrived in a chilled silver bucket, J. Murry filled their glasses and proposed a toast: "To our good friend, Judge Royal Peabody, who has, in his wisdom, agreed to allow Lulu to plead guilty to a charge of involuntary manslaughter in exchange for a suspended sentence and fine." J. Murry beamed at Lulu as if he had just convinced the Reverend Ian Paisley to pray for the Pope.

Lulu set her glass down without even as much as a sip of the bubbly. "I'll not plead guilty to something I did not do," she said.

Both J. Murry and Tad stared open-mouthed at Lulu. J. Murry regained his composure first.

"Lulu, I know you are tired and have had a wretched night. You have lost your faith in the justice system, and probably with good reason. However, I point out that if you do not enter this plea there is a real probability that you will spend the rest of your days in a maximum security women's prison.

"Let me point out what the State is dying to prove", he continued. You were a frequent visitor to the apartment of the late Ace Landeuix, a known pimp and small time grifter. In fact, according to all of Ace's neighbors, you were his only visitor. The knife that killed him bears your fingerprints.

"The jurors will ask themselves, 'what would a pillar of New Orleans society be doing when she regularly meets with a pimp in a dingy apartment. In their minds there could be only one answer. 'What was her motive for killing him?' they will ask themselves. Take your pick, a love affair gone sour, demands for money, threats to expose you. And finally they will ask themselves, 'If she did not kill him, why were her prints on the murder weapon,' Do you have an answer to that?" J. Murry stopped to catch his breath.

"I did go to his apartment for sex. I did pick up the knife that killed him. He was dead when I entered the apartment. But," her voice rose several octaves, "I did not kill the son of a bitch, and I will not say I did to keep my ass out of prison."

Both J. Murry and Tad recoiled. Never had they heard such language from this stunningly beautiful goddess.

Lulu went on, "I was born poor in a four-room shack over a bayou in south Louisiana. What I have acquired in life is what I've earned by my wits and good looks. I am not a fragile doll; I needed the love Ace gave to me. And, believe it or not, he was truly in love with me." She looked at them defiantly.

"We will do what we must do," J. Murry told her placing his hand on hers.

During the entire exchange Tad said not a word. His position in New Orleans society was threatened. He did not believe Lulu could love anyone, let alone scum like Ace Landeuix. So the whore-monger, card cheat, bust-out dice mechanic, and big-time grifter rose to his feet and walked away without looking back. Lulu knew she would not see him again. And, truly, she did not give a damn.

CHAPTER THIRTEEN

Late one night Ace was returning to his home after a gourmet meal of lox, roasted breast of duck, dirty rice, cajun style, and small bundles of asparagus bound together with bacon strips. The meal was complimented with vintage wine and finally with aged port.

As he exited Arnaud's he barely noticed a dirty, unshaven man sitting upon trash sacks in a dank, foul smelling alley. Since derelicts were not uncommon on the streets of Vioux Carre, Ace did not give it another thought. However, the hobo watched Ace with hooded eyes. Underneath the unkept beard and dirty face was Stan Griggs. At last, he thought, I have found the son of a bitch.

Griggs followed Ace to his home and then returned to the mission where he had been staying. He began to make dark and sinister plans.

CHAPTER FOURTEEN

J. Murry sat at his desk with his head in his hands. God help him, he truly believed her. But the evidence against her was so overwhelming how could he convince a jury that Lulu Desmonde did not commit so vile a crime? He had only the word of a beautiful woman who had lived a double life. He concluded there was only one solution—bribe a juror.

Jury tampering was nothing new to J. Murry. The first step was to acquire a list of jurors who would be called to serve at the trial. This was easy. He had a friend in the office of the Clerk of Court. For a very few dollars he could obtain any record he wanted. However, the list was long and only twelve would be selected to serve. Nonetheless, it was a start.

After obtaining the list he dispatched his investigator, Pierre Lafayette, to obtain information about each. He wanted, among other things, his or her credit rating, debts, and whether or not any had ever appeared in any court. Were they married, single or divorced, how much did they pay in taxes, what was the condition of their neighborhood?

Were they or any family members charged with a crime at any time? If so, what were the outcomes? What were their general reputations in the community? Did he or she cheat on his or her spouse?

All of these matters were important to J. Murry because when it came down to a selection of a potential "sinker," or bribed juror, he must be certain that because of one thing or another the juror will accept his proposal.

Weeks passed. Pierre obtained mountains of information. There were 119 potential jurors. The affairs of each were scrutinized and carefully documented. Who would be vulnerable to an offer of a large amount of cash? If so, how much? J. Murry was a strong believer that each person has his price. It's simply a matter of pushing the right button.

After tedious study of the files of each potential juror, J. Murry selected ten as likely candidates for his skullduggery. However, since some, if not all, of the ten might escape selection to serve on Lulu's jury, he had a second list of viable candidates.

In the long weeks awaiting trial Lulu, had become a recluse. She did not see her friends, if, indeed, any of her acquaintances could be called friends. She had not seen Tad since he walked away from her meeting with J. Murry at the Court of Two Sisters. She had not appeared at her boutique in weeks. It was during this very dark period in her life that she realized that other than her family, with whom she had not communicated since she left the swamp, her only friend in the world was J. Murry LaDeaux. He called upon her daily. They chatted about many things other than the upcoming trial. J. Murry always conveyed to her delicious gossip and rumors of affairs. She told him about growing up on the bayou. And when she talked about it, it seemed much more pleasant than it really was. She recalled the Cajun trappers and their love of life and family.

"Do you think I could ever go back?," she asked J. Murry on more than one occasion.

"Of course you can," J. Murry assured her, "and I will take you there."

This almost made her giggle. In her mind's eye she could see J. Murry in his frocked coat and silk shirt sculling a jonboat through a bayou. He no longer belonged there than she did in New Orleans. She had done her best to conform to the mores of her city cousins. Now she realized she was a round peg trying to fit herself into a square hole. Some things simply do not work. She did not realize how unhappy she was until her arrest and ostracism by the group of debutantes whom she had once counted as friends. No, once this ordeal was over she would return to the swamps and bayous of south Louisiana where she would find true happiness.

J. Murry was not really a bad guy. He was raised in a household devoid of any love or affection. His father's one passion was to make more money. His sugar mills flourished as did his huge fields of cane, cotton and rice. He owned his own cotton gins and rice dryers. J. Murry's mother was a member of New Orleans society, belonging to garden clubs, country clubs, bridge clubs and every other kind of club in existence. Neither had time for their only child who was raised by a series of nannies. When he finally found himself and became a lawyer neither parent seemed to notice. He often fantasized himself as Sydney Carton, ready to climb the steps of the guillotine so as to atone for past sins and to bring happiness to his true love. Having been raised by a family without ethics, J. Murry had no ethics himself. He took to bribing jurors, witnesses and even judges with no regrets. He hated convention as much as the devil hates martyrs.

He had no real friends, only those attracted to him by his money, his status or his reputation as a lawyer who could get things done. And this is what attracted him to Lulu. Although one started at the bottom and the other at the top of society, they had succeeded despite overwhelming odds against each of them. It was true that neither had used ethical methods in attaining their goals. And when they arrived they were unsatisfied and unfulfilled. They were truly kindred spirits.

On the day trial commenced J. Murry and Lulu entered into the courtroom. Lulu was frightened as she had never been frightened before.

Shortly after they entered, the bailiff directed all to stand and then began: "Here ye, hear ye, the District Court of Orleans Parish is now in session. All who have business draw near and ye shall be heard. God save these United States and this Honorable Court."

In his flowing black robe the judge entered into the court room and seated himself behind the bench. He surveyed the courtroom before saying, "You may be seated."

Judge Peabody had recused and the stern faced man behind the bench was the Honorable Judge Felix Blackman. He had an unruly mop of white hair and bushy eyebrows that also were snow white. He looked as if he had been weaned on a pickle. Lulu thought of an old adage of her father and decided she had rather be standing in the rain holding a mule than be here in Judge Blackman's courtroom.

Young Willie Wharton looked as somber as a pall bearer, wearing a black suit, starched white shirt and colorless tie. He was twenty five years of age but appeared to be no older than eighteen. His ego was still bruised by the refusal of Judge Peabody to incarcerate Lulu without bond.

"Is the defendant present?" asked Judge Blackman.

Rising to his feet, J. Murry answered, "Yes, your honor."

"Who appears for the State?"

In a rush to get to his feet Young Willie spilled a large stack of papers from the table in front of him. "Y. William Wharton, III," Young Willie finally stammered.

"Who is here on behalf of the defendant?"

Still standing, J. Murry identified himself.

"Is the State ready for trial?"

"Yes, sir, it is," spoke young Willie.

"Is the defense ready?"

"Yes, your Honor."

"Very well," said Judge Blackman. Turning to his bailiff he directed him to bring in the jury.

The prospective jurors entered through a door to the rear of the courtroom. There were twenty-four of them. Of the jury panel roster reviewed by J. Marry, two on his first list had survived this far and one on his second.

"Ladies and Gentlemen," commenced Judge Blackman, "twelve of you will be selected to serve on a jury to determine the guilt or innocence of a young woman charged with the second degree murder of one Ace Landeuix some six months ago. Those chosen will decide, after hearing the evidence produced by counsel and the law as instructed by me, whether the State has proven her guilty beyond a reasonable doubt or not. This is a grave responsibility and is not to be taken lightly. If you convict there will be a second trial to address the punishment to be handed out.

"The first phase of this trial, or any trial, is voir dire. From the Latin it means 'to speak the truth'. I will ask you some questions and then the attorneys will be permitted to ask other questions of you. No one will try to embarrass you. If you have a matter you would prefer that no one hears other than the Court or the lawyers, tell me and you may come forward to talk with us. This is what we call a bench conference.

"Has anyone heard or read anything about the alleged murder?" Since it had been in every newspaper south of Baton Rouge for the past six months and a daily report on radio and television, all were aware that a murder had been committed.

There were twenty four-raised hands. To the entire panel, Judge Blackman asked, "Have any one of you made up your mind regarding the guilty or innocence of Lulu Desmonde?"

Four hands were raised. Judge Blackman questioned each carefully and concluded that each had preconceived notions of Lulu's guilt and hence none could serve as an unbiased juror. They were released. None were on either of J. Murry's lists.

"Is everyone here a registered voter?"

There were no responses.

"Do you speak the English language?"

Although several of them were bilingual, all spoke English.

"Are any of you doctors, nurses or practitioners of the healing arts?"

Again, no responses. "Very good," said Judge Blackman. "Now, do any of you have any physical problems that would keep you from sitting as jurors?"

Three hands were raised. One older man had hearing aids in each ear and the judge excused him. In fact, he was forced to practically shout his excuse to him. Another had a bad back and was excused. A lady who tended to her invalid mother was also excused. J. Murry breathed a sigh of relief. None of his potential sinkers had sought exclusion. Of the original twenty-four, twenty-one were left.

"The State may began its voir dire," Judge Blackman decreed.

Young Willie practically leaped out of his chair. "May it please the Court," he commenced, looking in the direction of the Bench. Judge Blackman nodded.

He began with the usual questions asked by an attorney for the State. Such as whether the juror or a member of his family had ever been charged with a crime, was there anything about the justice system they distrusted, where did they worship, what clubs or lodges were they members of and the like. Young Willie went on and on. Finally he told them he anticipated the Court would instruct them as to the meaning of reasonable doubt. Not trusting his memory, he read from his file: "Reasonable doubt is not a mere or imaginary doubt. It is a doubt that arises from your consideration of the evidence and one that would cause a careful person to pause and hesitate in the graver transactions of life. A juror is satisfied beyond a reasonable doubt if after an impartial consideration of all the evidence he has an abiding conviction of the truth of the charge." Young Willie slammed his file shut and asked the jury, "Do you understand that instruction and can you abide with it?"

Most of the jurors' brains were numb from Young Willie's barrage of questions so they merely nodded their assent. J. Murry was pleased. Young Willie had demonstrated to the jury his total ineptness to try the lawsuit.

J. Murry, who already knew more about each juror than most of their family members, arose and in his deep baritone voice announced to the Court, "All of these fine people are acceptable to defendant. I will be proud to have any one of them serve. Therefore, I have no questions." He asked no questions because he knew if he could not find and recruit a sinker his case was lost.

All members of the jury panel breathed a collective sigh of relief. "What a nice man," they told themselves.

Judge Blackman directed the Bailiff to draw eighteen names from a box. Of the eighteen drawn, each side had three preemptory challenges. The twelve remaining would be the petit jury who would decide the case. The Bailiff began pulling names from the box and calling them to the clerk who wrote their names on a yellow pad. Of the eighteen names called, one was on J. Murry's first list and one on his second list. He was somewhat disappointed that Ruthie Gordon, an older black woman, was not selected. She lived from month to month on a small welfare check. She was so far behind in her rent she was about to be evicted. J. Murry knew that she wanted to be selected so she could earn the daily thirty dollar juror fee paid by the Parish. He made a mental note to send Pierre over to see her with a couple of hundred dollars. She might be a juror in another one of his cases. However, if Young Willie did not strike Buster McGee, he knew he had his sinker.

Buster McGee was a one-eyed longshoreman. He was ill-tempered and mean. He gambled and was heavily in debt to a loan shark. His wife had divorced him years ago. When he left the docks at the end of his shift he always migrated to Lefty McGinty's Bar and Grill. The only part of Lefty's that could qualify for the "Grill" part of the name was a large jar filled with green pickled eggs. He drank shots and beer until he either passed out or was broke. When he passed out fellow revelers dragged him to the rear of the building where he slept it off on dank blankets on the floor. He was the perfect juror for J. Murry.

Judge Blackman excused all for a late lunch. They were to be back in the courtroom at 2:30 p.m. The lawyers were instructed to decide their preemptory strikes during the lunch break and advise the Bailiff of such strikes before the 2:30 p.m. deadline for jurors.

J. Murry and Lulu did not eat lunch at all. Rather they studied the short list of the jurors from which they could strike three without giving a reason to the Court. They decided to strike none of the four black prospective jurors for two reasons. First, they were, as a general rule, more understanding regarding issues of morality. Second, and more important, was the fact that Young Willie might share their observations and use the three strikes allotted to him to eliminate three of the four blacks. Rather, they agreed to strike Shirley Barnes, a young woman with young children, because they recognized that she could be prudish as to matters of the heart; Rupert Tucker, an old preacher, for obvious reasons, and Bessie Blake, the manager of a down-and-out rooming house. J. Murry knew in his own mind that it really did not matter whom they struck because the evidence against Lulu was so overwhelming as to make an acquittal impossible unless Buster McGee was not struck by the prosecution and would be agreeable to accepting a bribe.

They returned to the courtroom early and nervously awaited the arrival of Judge Blackman. When he had taken his customary seat behind the bench, he directed counsel to deliver their respective strikes to the Bailiff. After they had done so, Judge Blackman directed the Clerk to read the names of the jurors who would try the case and seat them in the jury box in the order in which their names were called.

J. Murry almost shouted for joy when Buster McGee was seated as the 11th juror.

Judge Blackman himself swore the jury to well and faithfully try the case. He then excused them with instructions to be back ready to go to work at 9:30 the following morning. The lawyers rose to their feet as the jury left the courtroom.

After the jury had wandered out of the courtroom, J. Murry told Lulu, "Go home, mon cheri. I have work to do."

Then he left to direct Pierre to proceed to Lefty's Bar and Grill with an envelope full of cash. It was important that Pierre accomplish his purpose that night because the outcome would dictate how he would make his opening statement to the jury the following day.

CHAPTER FIFTEEN

Strangely enough, Sally Sue's affection for Ace, formerly Wilbur, grew with the years. Many years ago she decided that the whole thing was her fault. In her mind, he fled Wahoo because of his great fear of her father. And this she could understand. All of her life Simon had bullied and badgered her. She was an unwed mother living with her ten-year-old son under Simon's roof. She truly believed that her lover would some day return to her and take her to a happy home where the three of them would be a family.

Then one day she read in a Omaha newspaper of the brutal killing of a person known as Ace Landeuix. As she scanned the article a sentence caught her eye which caused her to read and re-read that one sentence. It simply said that he was wearing a diamond encrusted gold cross on a gold chain which, because of its delicate cast, appeared to have been made for a woman. Could this Ace Landeuix be one and the same as her beloved Wilbur Hunnicutt? Was the diamond cross that had been her mother's only article of jewelry the one stolen from her father's safe? If the body was not Wilbur's, then how did Ace Landeuix acquire the necklace?

She re-read the article again. The man had been beaten with a bull whip. Then she recalled that one day she noticed her father's bull whip, which had always hung in their barn, was gone. When she asked him about it he told her it had been stolen. He went on to say, "When I catch the bastad who stole from me, I'll come down on his so hard that he'll not steal again."

The victim was killed by a knife which the newspaper referred to as a long pointed knife. Simon had such a knife. He always kept it in a dresser drawer carefully oiled and honed. She felt an odd sensation in the pit of her stomach. Simon was in the fields directing the harvest of wheat and she was alone in their house. Should she look in the drawer?

If the knife was gone, what was she to do? She poured a tumbler of Simon's brandy into a sniffer and drank it down without savoring its aroma. She needed courage. Finally she braced herself, walked to Simon's bedroom and opened the dresser drawer. She did not see the knife. She frantically turned over the contents of the drawer until she was finally satisfied that the knife was gone. Then she held her head in her hands and wept. Could Wilbur be dead at Simon's hand? But wait, she asked herself. Even if the killer had gone to New Orleans from Simon's ranch, could it have been Silas who murdered her former lover, if indeed, the murdered man was Wilbur? Silas had more incentive to kill Wilbur than Simon. She had watched Silas through the years and knew of his deep, but unspoken, feelings for her. Silas could have stolen the whip as Simon had told her. He could have also stolen Simon's long knife. Silas had left the ranch two days before Wilbur's death and had not been seen or heard from since. Which ever one, if either, who may have been in Wilbur's death, had no effect on her life in Nebraska. She tucked her thoughts in a quiet corner of her mind and forgot about them. Sally Sue was unaware that a dirty, ragged Stan Griggs may have entered into their home unnoticed or she may have suspected Griggs to be the killer.

CHAPTER SIXTEEN

Pierre strolled into Lefty's Bar and Grill, selected a seat at the bar, and ordered a brandy. When told in no uncertain terms that Lefty's did not serve brandy, he ordered rye whiskey up. Although the rye was not the same smooth brand to which Pierre was accustomed, he sipped it gingerly, his eyes surveying the room. Soon his gaze came to rest on Buster McGee seated a few bar stools over. It was obvious that Buster was intent on spending his entire thirty dollar juror's fee before he left the bar. After a few minutes Pierre walked behind Buster's stool. He asked, "Pardon me, sir, but have we met before?"

Without looking up, Buster growled, "No."

"But," said Pierre, "I feel certain that we have met somewhere before."

Buster swung around on his bar stool and glared at Pierre. "What the hell are you, a queer or somethin'?"

Nonplused, Pierre went on, "Ah, Now I know you. You are one of the jurors in the Desmonde case."

Buster looked at him with his pale blue bloodshot eye, and told Pierre, "I know who you are. You're the bastard that went back and forth to that hot shot lawyer who thinks he can get the rich bitch off. Well, let me tell you here and now she's guilty as hell and will fry if I have my way."

"Of course, my friend. May I buy you a drink?"

Buster, never ever having turned down a free drink, nodded, looked at Nate, the bartender, and pointed to his empty shot glass. Nate took a bottle of rot gut whiskey from behind the bar and refilled the shot glass. He then drew a draft beer and set in front of him. Buster swallowed the shot, drained the glass of beer and looked at Pierre. Even in his whiskey soaked brain he doubted this flunky for the highfalutin lawyer would buy him anything simply because he was a nice guy.

"Another?" asked Pierre.

Buster nodded his assent and Nate went through the same ritual.

It was now obvious, even to Buster, why Pierre was buying him drinks. And he liked it.

"Let's go to a booth," suggested Pierre, "so we can talk in private."

Buster agreed and they went to a small booth in a dark corner of the bar.

"Mr. McGee," commenced Pierre, "I believe you know why I am here."

Before answering, Buster waived to Nate who brought him another shot and beer. "I reckon it's 'cause your boss wants to walk that bitch," he said.

"My friend, Ms. Desmonde is not guilty of any crime. However, it is important that we be assured of a friendly juror who can assist us," said Pierre.

"Let's git one thing straight. You ain't my friend but I might help you if the price is right," retorted Buster.

"Okay, let us lay our cards on the table. On behalf of my principal I am prepared to pay you $10,000 to hang the jury; $50,000 if you can secure an acquittal; $5,000 up front; and the balance when the verdict is returned."

Buster almost swallowed his tongue. However, he kept a straight face and asked, "Who's your principal?"

"I am not at liberty to say," answered Pierre. "If you wish to accept my proposition tell me and I will advance you the $5,000. If not, tell me so I can leave this rats' nest."

"Put your money where your mouth is," said Buster.

"Then it is agreed?" asked Pierre.

"Yeah."

Pierre reached into the inside pocket of his suit coat and produced a brown envelope.

He laid his hand on the envelope and said, "The money is in here. But before you take it, know that I have recorded our conversation. I carefully led your words to reach the end sought by me. If for any reason you should fail to honor our agreement the tape will be edited to make it appear that you came to me and offered to sway or hang the jury. And it will be sent to the police. Do you understand?"

Buster, who could not recall what had been said, nodded his assent. "Why give up the rest of my money?"

Nodding his head, Pierre removed his hand from the envelope. "Be sure to be in court promptly Monday," Pierre told him as he took his leave.

Outside the bar, Pierre spoke into his cell phone to J. Murry, "A okay." J. Murry hung up without saying a word.

CHAPTER SEVENTEEN

The trial commenced promptly at 9:30. Young Willie commenced his opening statement: "Ladies and Gentlemen of the jury, the purpose of opening statement is to tell you what the State will prove in its prosecution of Lulu Desmonde . . ."

Young Willie then identified each and every one of the witnesses who would be called upon to testify by the State. They included all six of the uniformed policemen, together with Alex Boudin and Claude Love, who were at the scene after the crime had been discovered. He called each by name and gave a narrative of their anticipated testimony. He next named the fingerprint experts and the forensic crew present and narrated what evidence would be offered by each. Next would be the pathologist who performed the autopsy. Then he would call in succession twelve of the tenants of the apartment house. Again he named them and gave an account of each's testimony.

At this point in Young Willie's opening statement the noon hour arrived and the jury was excused until 2 o'clock. They appeared to be in a zombie-like state.

At two o'clock Young Willie continued. He would call the undertaker who would testify to the grossness of the wounds on Ace's body. Insofar as the State could determine, Ace Landeuix had no family and hence no family member would be called.

He would introduce into evidence the bull whip and the long knife, bearing the finger prints of Lulu Desmonde, used to finish the job of murdering Ace. He would call Josh McDougald, the fingerprint expert who would testify that the knife bore the finger prints of the defendant. In addition, the jury would see the diamond-encrusted gold cross and chain Ace was wearing as well as his ripped and bloody clothes. Photographs of the body and the bloody apartment would be introduced.

Young Willie reminded the jury of the definition of reasonable doubt and the burden of proof that is placed upon the State. He submitted to them that not only would the State prove its case beyond a reasonable doubt but also beyond *any* doubt.

He then attempted to close his opening statement with a bit of humor. He told the brain-dead jury, "I don't know what kind of proof Mr. LaDeaux will offer. The only reasonable explanation that Ms. Desmonde may present is that Ace beat himself almost to death with a bull whip and then drove a large knife into his brain."

His attempt at humor was not well-received. As if with a single mind, all save Buster McGee, each juror wondered whether they could come up with any reason whatsoever to find against the wretched little man. Buster already had a reason.

The Judge excused the jury for their afternoon break. When they returned Judge Blackman looked at J. Murry and stated reluctantly that he could commence his opening statement.

J. Murry addressed the jury with slow deliberation: "Ms. Desmonde is innocent of any criminal act. Although it is not her burden, we will prove beyond any doubt whatsoever that she did not commit this dastardly crime. Keep an open mind until you have heard all of the evidence and then, I am sure, you will return a verdict of not guilty. Thank you."

Judge Blackman consulted his gold pocket watch. It was 3:30. He addressed the jury: "We are now proceeding into the next phase of the trial, which is testimony from witnesses. However, since it is late Friday afternoon I am going to excuse you until 9:30 Monday morning. I remind you that you are not to discuss this case with anyone, not even your spouse. If anyone tries to discuss the case with you, walk away and come to me. I will deal with him or her. I do not like to sequester a jury but will not hesitate to do so if one irregularity appears."

The jury left the courtroom. J. Murry closed his briefcase and walked briskly from the court house.

CHAPTER EIGHTEEN

The Omaha newspaper had been devoting a good deal of space to the trial in New Orleans. It was not that the trial was so newsworthy, but at the time there was little else to peak the interest of the readers than a juicy murder trial.

So when Sally Sue read the paper on Saturday morning, the events of the whip and the knife returned to her thoughts. She could not get her mind off the necklace. Could it have been her mother's? Was the bloody corpse in New Orleans actually that of Wilbur Hunnicutt?

The article identified Claude Love as the detective in charge of the investigation. Should she call him? If she did, what would she tell him? Should she implicate herself and her father or Silas in a trial hundreds of miles away?

After a morning of indecision Sally Sue obtained the telephone number of Police Plaza in New Orleans. Twice she began to dial and twice she stopped. Finally, summoning up all of her courage she called.

"One Police Plaza," a male voice spoke, "What may we do for you?"

Receiving no reply the voice spoke again. "Are you there?"

"May I speak with Detective Love?" she asked in a timid voice.

"What is the nature of your business?," he asked her.

"I may have information on the Desmonde case," she told him. "May I please speak with him?"

"And whom should I say is calling?"

Sally Sue hung up the phone. Her hands were trembling.

As the desk sergeant hung up the phone, Claude walked through the station. It was 9 o'clock in the morning. He told Claude of the call.

Claude was furious. "Why did you not put her through to me?"

"All I did was ask her to identify herself," the sergeant defended himself.

"Call the telephone company. Trace the call," Claude ordered.

Within a very few minutes Claude had the telephone number of one Simon Neathercutt in Wahoo, Nebraska. Claude dialed the number.

"Hello," came the answer of what evidently was the shaking voice of a young woman.

"This is Detective Claude Love in New Orleans. I am sorry that you were not put through to me immediately. Please forgive us," Claude commenced.

"The gold cross he was wearing when you found him—are there initials on the back?," she asked almost afraid to get an answer.

"Yes, there are initials," responded Claude. This was a bit of information withheld from the press so as to head off some crank calls.

She asked in a trembling voice, "Are they P.N.?

"Yes, my dear, that is exactly what they are. Is it yours?," Claude asked.

"It was my mother's. It was stolen from my father's safe ten years ago."

"Was the thief identified?" Claude asked.

"We believe it was Wilbur Hunnicutt," she told him.

"Can you describe him?" Claude asked.

She told him, "At the time he was nineteen. Handsome as a Greek god. Tall, slender, coal black hair and clear blue eyes."

"Did he have a small crescent scar on his left thumb?" Claude asked.

He heard a muffled sob and a faint "yes." Then she hung up.

Claude stared at the dead telephone. He hung up, got a new dial tone and called the number of J. Murry LaDeaux.

CHAPTER NINETEEN

After Claude and J. Murry talked, they agreed that even though it was Saturday morning a conference with Judge Blackman was in order. They found him on the tenth green at the Twin Oaks Country Club. Seeing the urgency on their faces, the Judge left his golfing companions and he, Claude and J. Murry went directly to the clubhouse.

Claude told Judge Blackman, "We have now identified the body as one Wilbur Hunnicutt, late of Wahoo, Nebraska. I believe we have a viable suspect other than Ms. Desmonde. We intend to immediately go to Nebraska to interview the prospective witness. If the trial proceeds as scheduled it could result in a gross miscarriage of justice."

"Why wasn't I told of this earlier?," asked Judge Blackman.

"Because we had no positive identification of the victim," Claude told him. "The finger prints taken post mortem matched the fingerprints of Ace Landeuix. However, the fingerprints on file at Police Plaza were made after Ace Landeuix arrived in New Orleans. In my heart I knew he must have had a past that would bear looking into before he arrived here. This is the first break we have had. Despite the evidence against her, never have I really believed Ms. Desmonde to be guilty."

Judge Blackman studied them soberly. Then he spoke, "Out of my great respect for you, Claude, and for no other reason, I am going to continue the trial for two days. But if this is a wild goose chase your asses will belong to me."

They pumped his hand vigorously before departing in a cloud of exhaust smoke for the airport. Neither had a change of clothing, toothbrushes or razors. However, these things could be purchased when they arrived at their destination. They barely made the 11:40 flight.

They arrived at the Omaha airport Saturday afternoon where they rented a car and began the short trip to Wahoo. The "Neathercutt

Place" was easy to find. It was as breathtaking to them as it had been to Silas years before. Standing high on a hill it commanded a view of green fields, carefully tended rows of wheat and soybeans and four clear blue ponds. A giant herd of whiteface cattle grazed peacefully in the pastures. It was picture-book perfect.

Simon himself answered the knock on his door. He looked at them without warmth.

Claude and J. Murry introduced themselves and explained their business. Simon's face darkened. He thundered to them, "I don't know what the hell you're talkin' about. Now git your butts offon my land 'afore I call the sheriff."

They were dumbfounded. "But, sir," said Claude, "we have found your late wife's necklace." He pulled it from his pocket and showed it to Simon.

"Never seen it before," said Simon almost shouting. "Now git!"

They slowly turned and walked to their car. "What are we going to do?" asked J. Murry. "If we try to go back the old bastard will probably kill us and the sheriff will give him a medal for protecting his property against trespassers."

"I don't know what we will do next," said Claude, "But I do know I will not be leaving here until I get some answers."

Simon's General Store was not open past noon on Saturdays. Since it was the only store in town they had no choice but to return to Omaha where they purchase clothing and toilet articles. Having noticed a Bed and Breakfast in Wahoo they returned once again and checked in. It was after 10 o'clock and both fell into a deep and dreamless sleep. It had been a long and tiring day.

Early the next morning the telephone in the room rang. Looking at his watch before he answered the phone Claude saw it was 7 a.m.

"Hello," he said into the phone stifling a yawn.

"Is this Detective Love?" asked a vaguely familiar voice.

Claude was immediately alert. The voice was certainly that of his caller from the Neathercutt residence of yesterday. "It is," he said, "and how may I help you?"

"I have information that will help you in your murder investigation," she answered.

"Who is this?," asked Claude.

"I am Sally Sue Neathercutt, Simon's daughter. Wilbur is the father of my child. When I learned of the murder I was uncertain whether it was committed by Silas, one of our field hands, or my father. Both hated him with a vengence. After you left yesterday Simon was in a terrible rage. He beat me and told me if I talked with you again he would kill me."

"When and where can we talk?" asked Claude.

"Nine o'clock behind the First Baptist Church," she instructed him.

Claude and J. Murry were waiting at the designated place when Sally Sue arrived.

"God in heaven," gasped Claude.

Both of her eyes were black, one swollen almost shut. It appeared that her nose had been broken and there were bruises were on her arms and legs.

"Did he did your father do this to you, child?," asked Claude in a low voice, almost a whisper.

"Yes," she replied, "but do not concern yourselves with me. I will tell you the whole story, starting when Wilbur arrived in Wahoo and ending today."

And she began relating the whole sordid tale, from her relationship with Wilbur to his robbing Simon and fleeing in the night. She related Silas' unfilled love for her. Both Simon and Silas became obsessed with revenge against Wilbur. Simon hired private detectives to attempt to locate the elusive Wilbur. During a ten-year period his search was relentless.

After his wife died, Simon would periodically go to Omaha for a few days where he would drink and enjoy the company of whores. He was gone the day before and after the day after Wilbur's death.

Then she told them of the missing whip and knife. She told them her mother's necklace had been stolen by Wilbur. At this point, she firmly believed that the killer resided at the Neathercutt ranch. But was it her father or Silas?

She went on to tell them after they left Simon's house he came into her room in a rage. He cursed her and beat her. He shouted that if she ever talked to anyone again about Wilbur Hunnicutt he would kill her. She believed him and armed herself with Simon's pistol. Earlier that morning he had come into her room in a drunken stupor. When he drew back his arm to strike her again she shot him in the forehead.

"I'm not sorry," she said. "He was a mean man without pity or remorse. The world is better off with him out of it."

Claude placed a hand on her shoulder. "Bless you. It has been a hard life. Now we must go to the sheriff and report what happened."

"I called the sheriff at three this morning. He and his forensic crew were at our house until shortly before I called. He told me everyone in the county is better off. He must report to the prosecuting attorney, but he does not believe charges will be filed."

"Were Simon's initials scratched on his knife?"

"Yes," she answered.

"And did he confess to the murder to you?"

"In his drunken stupor he raved about the hatred he and Silas had for Wilbur and how he had his revenge I believe that one or both of them killed him."

"There is a woman in New Orleans who has been unjustly charged with this murder. Will you be agreeable to signing an affidavit attesting to the matters you have just told us so the charges against her can be dismissed?" asked Claude.

"Of course," she answered. "No one should suffer on account of what those evil men did."

And so the three of them went to the office of a notary public where J. Murry dictated the affidavit that would set Lulu free. After she signed it and the notary attested to it, J. Murry and Claude returned to New Orleans.

CHAPTER TWENTY

Claude and J. Murry sat in front of Judge Blackman, who studied the affidavit. "Is it true that the initials S.N. were scratched on the blade of the murder weapon?" he asked Claude.

"It is true. I also have an affidavit from Gaston Hebert, the private investigator who located Ace for Simon, at a very great cost, I might add." He handed the affidavit to the Judge.

Since none of this had ever seen Hebert, none knew that he was a bearded man with a scar on his cheek that shown white in contrast to his black beard. Was he the same man the barkeep saw accepting a legal document from Stan Griggs? No one will ever know.

Judge Blackman slowly and carefully read the Hebert affidavit. "What do you want me to do?," he asked.

"Dismiss the charges," Claude and J. Marry spoke as one.

"Very well," said Judge Blackman. Then to J. Murry he directed, "Bring me an Order of Dismissal."

"Your Honor," said J. Murry, "I took the liberty of already drafting one." He produced the document from his briefcase and presented it to the Judge.

Smiling slightly, Judge Blackman signed the order and returned it to J. Murry who clutched it as if it were the keys to heaven.

CHAPTER TWENTY ONE

Upon his arrival back at his office J. Murry found Pierre waiting for him. "Buster McGee was arrested," a solemn-faced Pierre related to J. Murry.

"Whatever for?," he asked.

"Well," Pierre told him, "he had been scattering one hundred dollar bills like autumn leaves at Lefty's. The police could not believe that he came by such money honestly so they arrested him on suspicion of having committed a crime. Old Buster kept insisting that he had won the money gambling. Since no citizen complained to being robbed or the like they finally let him go."

J. Murry rolled back his head and roared with laughter.

"Give him another five thousand," he instructed Pierre.

"But why, he didn't do anything to earn it," Pierre countered.

"Because I said to do so, that's why,' J. Murry told him in a stern voice. "The little hustler could have reported me to the bar ethics committee. And that would have been all she wrote. Not only would I have lost my license but also I could have been charged under a federal statute for jury tampering."

Pierre nodded his assent.

CHAPTER TWENTY TWO

As soon as the criminal charges were dismissed against Lulu, the socialites once considered by Lulu as friends began calling her. She refused to take their calls or to return them. However, Lulu continued to see J. Murry on a daily basis.

One afternoon, while sitting on Lulu's veranda, she told J. Murry, "I've decided to go back to south Louisiana. As my attorney I want you to sell my business and my house. Liquidate all of my other assets and put it all in a trust for the benefit of me, my parents and my brothers and sisters. Provide an allowance for each of us and reinvest the money received from the trust not expended for our allowances back into the trust."

"But where will you go?," asked a devastated J. Murry.

She laughed without humor. "Do not concern yourself, I'll not return to my parents' shack in the bayou. I intend to build a small house near Grand Isle and get my life back together."

J. Murry told her in a voice that choked, "I cannot live without you. All of my life I have taken and not given. Please don't leave me. I'll go to Grand Isle with you. We'll fish, go shrimping, set crab traps. I would die for you, Lulu."

"Then live for me," she said. "You and I both know you are not suited for life in the swamps. However, I'll make a deal with you. You may visit me in Grand Isle from time to time. If you adapt to such a way of life then perhaps we can place it on a more permanent basis."

And J. Murry, known from New Orleans to Miami as a cold blooded, heartless bastard without emotion, hung down his head and wept for pure joy.

CHAPTER TWENTY THREE

Claude is really never quite so happy as he is when he pieces a puzzle together. Of the three persons who could relate the circumstances of their confrontation, Ace and Simon, were dead, and Silas had disappeared. So a recreation of the events was left to imagination. Claude's mind envisioned what truly happened that fateful day which forever changed the lives of Lulu Desmonde, Ace Landeuix and Tad McJunkin. Had he known of Stan Griggs, he would most probably put him at the top of his list of the identity of the killer. What he did not know was that Stan was arrested for public intoxication the same night Stan had found Ace. Stan was serving a thirty day sentence in the Parish jail when the murder took place.

Claude wrote in his notebook, as if he had been there, the following account.

When Ace entered his studio apartment for his weekly tryst with Lulu, his eyes bugged out and his throat became dry with fear and terror. An intruder was sitting in his easy chair with a bull whip in his right hand and a long knife in his left. Ace turned toward the door when the bull whip uncoiled, wrapping itself around Ace's ankles. The intruder dragged him into the room as if he were landing a large fish. He shut and locked the door as Ace rose to his feet.

The uninvited guest's eyes were flat and his voice, when he spoke, was cold and without inflection.

"You're pretty good at losin' yourself," Ace was told. "A barrel of money and a lot of time were spent findin' you. It was worth it."

Ace could feel cold sweat spreading from his armpits down his rib cage. "Now, wait," Ace pleaded. "It's all a misunderstanding. I can explain."

With that, intruder's right hand coiled and the bull whip snapped, opening a five inch-gash in Ace's cheek.

"Good God Almighty," Ace cried. "Don't hit me again. I've got money, lots of money. You can have it all."

With that the bull whip cracked again causing unbearable pain to Ace's rib cage. "I have friends on the police force. You can't get away with this." He was sobbing.

"Your friends and your money will do you no good you miserable pissant," Ace was told. "You're gona die."

Ace's lips peeled back in a terrible grimace. With a scream like a wounded buffalo he lunged across the room toward his antagonist. With a sick smirk on his face, the wrist of the oppressor flicked and the bull whip again wrapped itself around Ace's legs, spilling him to the floor.

With Ace's face to the floor he was coolly and deliberately beaten with the bull whip. His shirt was reduced to bloody tatters and his back was laced with lash marks. It was then that Ace realized he was going to die. His pain became so great that he was no longer able to cry out. He simply sobbed. Finally Ace's limp body was turned on its back. His killer pulled a long knife called an Arkansas Toothpick from a sheath on his belt and held it under Ace's chin long enough for him to realize what was happening. Then he jammed the twelve-inch blade through the bottom of his chin upward into his brain. Ace Landeuix was no longer.

The murderer wiped his fingerprints clean from his Arkansas Toothpick and his bull whip and left them in the small apartment. He then disappeared into the damp night.

Lulu arrived at the studio less than an hour after the killer had gone. She unlocked the apartment door with her own key and entered, calling Ace's name. Then she gasped, and open mouthed gazed at the floor. Although she was tough as nails, the sight of Ace's bloodied, mangled body caused Lulu to turn away in horror. In almost a stupor she picked up the knife that killed Ace. Used by river boatmen it was three inches in width next to its hilt, which tapered to a sharp point around twelve inches later. It was a great knife, good for repairing nets, shaving and cutting tough meat. It was also the river man's best friend and was used not infrequently in bar fights in Helena, Natchez Under the Hill and the red-light district of New Orleans.

Lulu flung down the knife and bolted for the door. In the hall she breathed deeply. Had anyone seen or heard her? She didn't think so.

She stood motionless for a full two minutes trying to tell whether she had been seen. Then satisfied she had not been detected, she slipped out of the hallway and into the evening air.

Claude turned the events over and over in his mind.

If it was not Simon, why would he have beaten Sally Sue so viciously? What would he have spent so much time and money to locate Wilbur if he didn't intend to avenge himself and his daughter?

On the other hand, could it have been Silas? If not, why did he vanish two days before the killing? Did his love sick mind snap and cause him to so brutally murder his rival?

Or could Silas and Simon have been in cahoots? Did Silas do the planning and Simon commit the deed? Or vise-versa?

Claude deduced that if Silas was never found, the identify of the real killer would never be learned. And most probably Silas would not be found. After all, no one was looking for him and he most probably would vanish as just another farm hand in some remote spot. But what the hell, wasn't New Orleans a better place without Ace. He sighed deeply and closed his notebook.

MEET MOON BOONE

A SHORT NOVEL

Most of the guys who hung around Fred's pool hall were convinced that Stonewall Jackson "Moon" Boone was not born but hatched from a giant egg laid by some poor female bird who had no idea what she was loosening on humanity. This is not to say that Moon was not likeable because he was. He was called "cuddly" by the girls who worked for Maxine at the rooms over the pool hall. Moon's sole purpose in life was to sell enough mail-order shoes so his mother would raise his allowance. This would enable him to rent one of Maxine's girls for half an hour or so.

Moon stood approximately 5'2" and weighed in the neighborhood of 250 pounds. His chubby face was framed in curly black locks that gave him the appearance of an archangel who was visiting the planet earth for a few days. He spent four of the happiest years of his life in the third grade at Westside Baptist School before even the preachers gave up trying to impart a little knowledge on Moon, much less basic math and bonehead English. When it became evident that he would never be passed from the third to the fourth grade, Moon put his academic endeavors behind him and commenced to engage in gainful employment.

Moon's father, Caleb Boone, had worked at Draper's Sawmill since he was no older than Moon was when Moon dropped out of school. It was preordained that Moon would follow in his father's footsteps in the sawdust littering the floor of Draper's. However, it was not to be. The first day on the job Moon sliced off a portion of his pinkie finger while attempting to operate the band saw. When he returned to work sporting a bandaged pinkie, he was assigned a forklift to drive. Less than an hour later Moon drove the lift of the machine through the roof of the sawmill, shutting down operations for three days. The last job Moon had at the mill was weighing trucks loaded with logs at the scale house. However, on account of his lack of academic skills, after one day the records of Draper's were so muddled that it took a team of CPAs to unravel the errors in the books of the scale house.

Mr. Draper called Caleb into his office. After offering coffee, he told Caleb, "Moon is not cut out for sawmill work. You have been a good employee for more years than both of us would like to think about and I'd do almost anything to accommodate you. However, Moon must go."

Caleb nodded his head in silent assent and left the room. It was going to be his unpleasant duty to inform his wife, Gertrude, of Moon's rejection from the mill.

After his tenure at the mill, Moon worked in succession at a service station, as a stable hand and as a paper boy. He was unable to change oil so the service station job was short-lived. Horses didn't like him and after receiving several kicks he was released, to his great satisfaction, from his employment as a stable hand. Because of his short attention span he was unable to keep track of to whom he should deliver newspapers.

While such setbacks would cause great despair to most, it was Moon's gentle spirit and happy outlook that kept him friendly and happy. Moon knew that a guardian angel looked after him and it was only a question of time before his future would be decided.

In keeping with the way angels work, Moon's life work appeared in a most unusual way. Moon was dozing on one of the chairs at the shoeshine stand in Fred's when he felt someone untying one of his shoes. He looked down to see an industrious young man loosening his shoelaces.

"Why are you untying my shoes?" asked Moon.

"Because", answered the lad, "I am about to sell you the handsomest, most economical shoes you have ever had the pleasure of wearing on your feet."

And, behold, there appeared from a satchel at the side of the young salesman a gleaming pair of black and white wing tips that boggled Moon's mind. Almost breathless with anticipation, Moon allowed the beautiful shoes to be planted on his size 7 EEE feet. It was then he knew he was hooked for life as a shoe peddler.

It did not take the sales manager of Beautiful Bipeds long to discover that Moon was not an Albert Einstein in performing even the simplest mathematical tasks. Therefore, Moon's sales kit consisted only of a catalog of shoes available and an order form. His customers simply completed the order form, gave him a check and the shoes would be promptly mailed to the purchaser. Moon's mother was delighted to complete the mailing of the orders and to receive Moon's monthly commission check, and to give him an allowance. Moon, happy as a hog in the sunshine, thrived on his new vocation. His customers were happy to buy a pair of cheap shoes to relieve themselves from Moon's incessant chattering.

However, into each life some rain must fall. Moon's rain came very unexpectedly in a communication from Beautiful Bipeds. Moon's mother read the message to him when he returned home from a particularly good day for sales. It said:

"Congratulations, Moon Boone. You have been chosen as salesman of the year by Beautiful Bipeds. As a reward for your excellent sales record you will be treated to a three-day trip to New York City. Included as your prize are round-trip airplane tickets from Little Rock to New York City, two nights at the Broadway Crown Plaza, an allowance of $300.00 for incidentals and a ticket for *Forty-Second Street!*. Enclosed are round-trip airplane tickets, a check for $300.00 for meals, confirmation for a two-day prepaid stay at the Crown Plaza and a *42nd Street*! ducat. Have a great time, Moon. Get your motor recharged and have an even better year next year."

Moon bit down hard on his lifesaver mint. Except for a five-day stint in the Marine Corps, he had never been farther away from home than Smackover. He must now travel through Smackover to Little Rock and then, wonder of wonders, to New York City. He would rather have stood in the rain holding a mule than to travel to New York City by way of Little Rock. But since he was the ace salesman he could not say "no."

Moon would be traveling alone and without a leader. While digesting the news in his pea-sized brain Moon concluded he would probably not reach New York, but, if he did, he would never return. Would he join that army of transients who slept under bridges, had few teeth and urinated outdoors? Would his successful sales career be terminated? Would he ever return to El Dorado?

Moon's mother packed his bag, placed all of his tickets and cash in a money belt, secured the belt around his large middle and drove him to the

Little Rock National Airport. She dropped Moon and his bag at the Delta counter at the airport and drove away in a cloud of exhaust smoke.

Firm in his belief that he was embarking on a one-way trip, Moon approached the Delta counter. He had his ticket and a passport that his mother had obtained for him since he could not pass the test for a driver's license. His bag was checked through at the curb and he received a boarding pass. Moon reached into his pocket, found a dime and tipped the red cap, who stared at him in confusion.

Holding his ticket in one hand and gripping his money belt with the other, Moon passed through the metal detector. As he crossed over, a burly man escorted him to a chair and commanded that Moon take off his shoes. "This is it," thought Moon, "I'm a dead man. I've seen this in the movies. He's going to make me walk on hot coals and then burn me at the stake. Why, oh why, did I leave on this trip?"

But to Moon's happy surprise his shoes were returned to him intact and he was directed to proceed to Gate 8. The walk from the metal detector to Gate 8 was down a long, straight hall making it impossible for Moon to get lost. When he arrived at Gate 8 he wearily presented his boarding pass to the ticket agent who glanced at it and told Moon to be seated. Moon took a seat next to a large hayseed wearing bib overalls. He longed for Fred's pool room and the never-ending prospects for shoe sales.

"Where you headin'?" asked Mr. Bib Overalls.

Moon stared straight ahead and spoke through clinched teeth, "New York City."

"Well, "said his new friend, "Ah'm goin' to Memphis, Dee-troit, Chicago, St. Louie, Los Angeles and San Francisco."

This peaked Moon's interest. "Why are you going to so many places?"

"To collect my welfare checks," Mr. Bib Overalls confided.

"Do you collect welfare in all of those places?" asked Moon.

"Yep, and here in El Dorado, Texarkana and Shreveport. They're so close I drive there in my new Cadillac. There's good money in Welfare. The secret is to have bunch of places where you kin git your money. One 'r two ain't near enough."

There was something about Mr. Bib Overall's business that didn't seem quite right to Moon. However, after turning it over in his mind he could see nothing wrong with it. Nonetheless, he much preferred selling shoes.

The ticket agent directed the passengers to commence loading. Moon did as he was directed and found that he had a center seat between a kindly looking older lady and a darkly tanned man wearing a turban who muttered to himself in a language Moon could not understand. Moon's roly-poly body was squeezed so tightly between his two traveling companions that he could scarcely breathe. He clutched the armrest so tightly his knuckles showed white. When the airplane arrived at its place in line to take off, Moon passed out. Fortunately his body was so crammed in between the other two passengers that neither realized he was doing anything but sleeping. Indeed, were it not for his snow white knuckles all would have believed he was resting in quiet repose.

The next thing Moon knew the kindly looking old lady seated in the window seat was poking him in the ribs saying, "Wake up, fat ass, we're here."

Short as Moon was, when poked in the ribs he jumped straight up striking his head so hard against the roof of the airplane that he was almost knocked unconscious again. Granny was unrelenting. "Get your butt out of my way or I'll have you for supper."

Moon's brain did not always respond as rapidly as he preferred. However, he leaped from his seat into the aisle landing on the foot of a well-dressed, kindly appearing older lady. She cursed him roundly while hitting him with her purse. All that Moon could think of was, "I'm going to be here two more days."

After deplaning without further incident, Moon located the baggage claim area.

There was good news and bad news at baggage claim. The good news was neither of the drug sniffing dogs had lifted a leg on his suitcase. The bad news was that he had gone to the wrong baggage claim area and consequently had no suitcase to claim. He was escorted to the unclaimed baggage area and after disclosing to the agent that there was a large rabbit foot in his bag he was allowed to take it without further ado.

He was directed to the taxi area where he patiently waited in line for a cab. Moon had no idea of the distance between LaGuardia Airport and downtown. Even further from his mind was the soon-to-be recognized fact that New York cab drivers speed through the streets like fugitives from a breakout at Cummins Prison. He was placed in a cab that took him to the Crown Plaza. The trip took half an hour during which time Moon aged a good five years. If you think that his knuckles were white on the airplane you should have seen them during the taxi ride. When they reached the toll booth on the Queensboro Bridge, Moon was in such shock that he could not unloosen his money belt to pay the toll. With a sigh, the driver paid it and sped toward downtown. The only other drive that had been so traumatic was when Moon's first cousin Sweetpea Joad got drunker than Cooter Brown and took Moon for such a violent ride through the woods on a four-wheeler that Moon vowed to never ride with Sweetpea again. This was a good thing because the following weekend Sweetpea was arrested for his fourth DWI within a year and sentenced to a year at Arkansas State Prison in Cummins.

Mercifully the cab arrived at the Crown Plaza. Moon was in such a state that the cab driver had to remove his money belt to be paid. He was uncertain as to the size of the tip the driver took but he was so elated to be out of the wretched taxi that the amount of the tip was totally irrelevant.

His receipt for two nights' lodging was accepted by the desk clerk without incident. "Things are looking better," Moon thought as he rode the elevator in an upward path. Safely in his room, Moon brushed his teeth, put on his pajamas, said his evening prayer and dropped off to a deep and dreamless sleep. He had survived day one.

Moon awoke before daylight. Looking out his window he was shocked to see such activity. People, cabs, policemen, street peddlers and the like were all going about their business. He showered, shaved and dressed. In the restaurant in the lobby he ate a breakfast at a cost which was enough to retire the debts of some third world countries. When he was allowed $300 for cabs and meals he believed he would return home with at least half that much left over. It became painfully obvious if he were to survive on the $300 allowance, his meals must be confined to diners.

While walking along Madison Avenue Moon was approached by a high-haired blond wearing a mini-skirt and a sweater that was undersized at least two sizes. "Want to have a good time, Baby?" the hooker asked.

Now she was speaking a language that Moon understood from his nocturnal visits at Maxine's House of Joy located over the poolroom. Moon assumed what he hoped was his most disarming pose and asked "How much?"

"Five Hundred," quoted the blond.

"Five hundred what?" Moon asked, believing he had misunderstood.

"Dollars, numbskull," she answered.

"Good-bye," said Moon and began walking away.

"Wait, baby," cried the blond. "For you, four hundred."

Moon lowered his shoulders and continued to walk away at a brisker pace. At least he had learned that New York was not the place to come with sex on your mind.

Continuing his walking through midtown New York, Moon's stomach reminded him that it was time for lunch. Passing Su-Ling's restaurant, Moon read the menu posted outside the door. Most of the entrees Moon could not understand. However, there was a dish called sushi that cost only $4.95. After being seated at a table Moon ordered sushi. When it was brought to him it looked like nothing he had ever seen before.

"What is sushi?" asked Moon.

"Raw fish," the pretty Oriental girl replied.

Moon leaped out of his chair, knocking his table over and spreading sushi throughout the area surrounding him. An elderly man dropped his chopsticks. A bewildered waitress watched while he exited the building as if he were being chased by Kamikaze pilots. He calmed his shattered nerves and finally settled on a hamburger at Friday's that cost $9.84.

Bored to tears, Moon decided to take a bus tour through parts of New York for the bargain price of $22. What impressed Moon the most was a trip through the Bowery which looked like the Thunder Zone at El Dorado. Homeless, toothless men and women, who obviously had not seen the inside of a bathroom for years, roamed the streets pushing shopping carts. Moon wished he could join them and escape the theater that evening.

His bus ride over, Moon returned to his hotel and put on his blue double knit suit, white shirt and Sears tie that glowed in the dark. The tie, Moon decided, added a touch of elegance to his otherwise drab trappings.

Sitting through *42nd Street!* with his mouth wide open, Moon felt as though he had entered another planet. The music, the songs, the dancing, the costumes thrilled Moon so that he almost decided to stay in New York and participate in such extravaganzas on musical Broadway. But then his deeper thoughts took over and he knew he must return to El Dorado to cater to his shoe customers. Anyway, Moon couldn't carry a tune in a bucket, which would be another minor but, he reasoned, not an insurmountable drawback to participation in a Broadway musical.

As he left the theater Moon was humming "I Only Have Eyes for you," and "We're in the Money," while doing a small jig. Moon felt so good that he wanted to do something more before returning to his hotel room. As he walked up Fifty Fourth Street he encountered a pool hall. Happily, Moon entered like he had returned home. Nothing, Moon decided, smells as good as a pool hall. Heavy tobacco smoke mingled with the aroma of cheap rye whiskey and pool chalk permeated the room. The leather covered sweater's chairs glistened with a sheen of new oil and emitted a subtle yet distinctive odor blended in with talcum powder, human sweat and steam heat. Moon sighed contentedly; he had found a home away from home.

When Moon walked through the door he was surveyed by an assortment of pool hustlers. What would you think of a hayseed wearing a double knit suit and a tie that glowed in the dark if you were a professional pool shark? The obvious—grab the rube, put a cue in his hand and clean his clock. This, however, was not to be. Moon had been fleeced so many times by ordinary players at Fred's that he knew he couldn't play with these guys. So he politely but firmly rejected all offers for a "friendly game." Indeed, he even declined the offer of one dressed in a hound's tooth sports coat with a huge diamond ring on his pinkie finger who offered to spot Moon the fifteen ball and play him left-handed.

Rather, he bought a coke for the huge price of $3, sank happily in a sweater's chair and watched the action. He felt a twinge of guilt for not bringing his catalog and order forms because he was in a rich area that needed harvesting. He was so relieved to be in the pool hall that he forgot all about dinner.

The pool hall closed at 2:00 a.m. When the last cue was cased and the last ball put away, Moon left for his hotel, tired but happy. On his way home he had to deal with two different hookers. He longed for Maxine's. "Well," he thought, "I'll be home tomorrow."

Moon slept until nine o'clock. He arose, shaved and showered in less than an hour. By ten o'clock he had checked out of the Crown Plaza and was bound for LaGuardia in a taxi driven by a large dark man of uncertain ethic background. If the drive coming in from the airport had been scary, this ride was downright frightening. Nonetheless, Moon persevered and was soon in front of the Delta terminal at the airport. He tipped the driver a whole dollar out of fear and proceeded to check his bag through to Little Rock. He gave the dismayed ticket agent a quarter for his trouble.

This time Moon was seated between two teenaged girls who has been to New York to visit a maiden aunt. Happily Moon exchanged his center seat for the aisle seat so the young ladies could squeal and gossip. Moon's spirits soared. He had withstood taxi rides from and to the airport, he still had $34.34 of his $300 left, and he had successfully fought off five pool hustlers and three hookers. The magic of *42nd Street!* was clearly visible in his mind's eye as were the happy hours spent in the pool hall. He nodded off into a blissful sleep. However, when the plane began its ascent Moon again almost jumped out of his skin.

The rest of the story of Moon's visit to New York was uneventful. His mother picked him up at the Little Rock airport and they motored safely home to El Dorado. Moon took the next day off, but the following morning he was happily present at Fred's.

As the days, then weeks, then months passed by, Moon's stories of the wonders of New York grew by leaps and bounds. The last one, I understand, places Moon with Lou Pinella and Rudy Gulianni at a Yankee's baseball game. He danced with the stars of not only *42nd Street!* but also *The Producers* and many others. He and Nathan Lane bonded into a lasting friendship.

However, Moon makes it very clear that he will not return. Why meddle with perfection?

MOON AND THE LAW

Moon had had no experience with the law or lawyers until he was summoned for jury duty before the Circuit Court of Union County, Arkansas. The sheriff arrived with the summons and gravely informed Moon that he had been summoned for jury duty and must be in court the following Monday. The expectation of watching real lawyers and judges left Moon breathless with anticipation. Between the date of his summons and his court appearance he slept only fitfully. In his dreams he saw giant images of the scale of justice and the descending gavel of a judge.

On the appointed day Moon arose early and put away his beloved shoe samples and order book. He dressed in his blue double knit suit, but forewent his Sears tie that glowed in the dark. Rather, he selected a black tie from his father's wardrobe. The selection was simple as Caleb, his father, owned only three ties, all black. Suitably attired and wearing his best pair of Beautiful Bipeds Moon exited his home and left for his great adventure.

Although the route between his home and Fred's Pool Hall was burned into his brain, Moon had walked only a block when he realized that he did not know the location of the courthouse. After wandering aimlessly for what seemed like a long while, he encountered a newspaper boy who was delivering his papers on his bicycle. Moon approached him and asked, "Can you tell me where the courthouse is?"

The boy, around age 13, looked at Moon with suspicion. "Don't you know nothing?", asked the small entrepreneur.

Moon, having no suitable answer, simply looked pleasantly at whom hopefully would be his guide.

"Aw, hell," said the kid, "go north on Timberlane for a block, turn east to Main and keep goin' 'till you git thair."

Moon was in a quandary. He did not know north from west, or east from south. "Could you point?" Moon asked.

The boy told him, "Look, I'll be deliverin' a newspaper to the courthouse so if you'll foller me I'll show you the way."

Moon commenced to follow him at a fast pace. However, his stubby legs were no match for the speed of the bicycle. His face grew red and his starched white shirt was beginning to melt when a patrol car of the El Dorado Police Department stopped.

"Is this man chasing you?" the policeman asked the newsboy.

"Naw," he said, "I'm showin' him the way to the courthouse."

"What business do you have at the courthouse?" the policeman asked Moon.

Moon, redfaced and sweating profusely, was unable to respond at once. He finally caught his breath and said "Jury duty."

Both cops then recognized Moon at the same time as the persistent salesman of mail order shoes. He had attempted on more than one occasion to interest both in investing in Beautiful Biped without success.

"Come on, Moon," said the taller, older one. We will drive you to the courthouse."

Moon got into the squad car through the rear door and immediately discovered that there was no inside door handle and that there was a heavy wire screen separating him from the front seat.

One policeman winked at the other, who turned on the siren and blue flashing lights atop the car and accelerated to break neck speed. Moon quaked in the back seat. The speed increased so rapidly that Moon was reminded first of his wild ride through the woods with his cousin Sweetpea Jeter on his four-wheeler and then of his frightening taxi rides in New York City.

Arriving at the courthouse one of the policemen opened the rear door for Moon, who practically fell out onto the ground. Without thanking his hosts, Moon dashed for the courthouse on wobbly legs.

In the courthouse a deputy sheriff asked Moon for his jury summons. Moon had held it in his clinched fist since leaving home and consequently it was a soggy mess. He delivered the summons to the deputy who did his best to unfold it and decipher the words on it. After squinting at the summons for an indeterminate length of time the deputy was convinced that Moon was a genuine prospective juror and escorted him into the jury room.

Upon entering into the jury room Moon spotted two familiar faces. One was Lulabelle from Maxine's House of Joy over Fred's Poolroom and the other was Mr. Bib Overalls, the welfare entrepreneur from the Little Rock airport. They were seated in straight backed chairs along all four walls of the large room housing the jury panel. There was a vacant seat beside Mr. Bib Overalls so Moon gratefully sank into it.

"I didn't know you lived in El Dorado," Moon stated.

"Yep, here and in all them other places where I collect my welfare checks," Mr. Bib Overalls told him.

"How do you keep track of all the places where you live," Moon asked.

"Depends on the day that the welfare checks are delivered," Mr. Bib Overalls told him.

Mr. Bib Overalls asked, "Ever sit on a jury before?"

"Nope, what about you?" Moon inquired.

"Oh, yeah," he answered, "Los Angeles, San Francisco and St. Louie. I was called to be on a jury in New York but they couldn't find me. The bastards cut off my welfare in New York." It was obvious no love was lost between him and the city of New York.

"Why did they cut off your benefits in New York?" Moon asked. He was perplexed. Why should Mr. Bib Overalls' benefits be cut off simply because he was not present in New York when summoned for jury duty?

"Because they are low lifed, stinkin' polecats," he told Moon. It was apparent Moon had touched a sensitive spot. He debating whether to pursue the subject further when the bailiff entered the room. All chatter stopped and forty-eight pairs of eyes focused on the bailiff. He was a short balding man who fantasized himself to be General George Patton, wearing his pearl handled pistol and causing all in his wake to cower in fear. He was obviously greatly impressed with himself and the power he held over the forty-eight souls in the jury room.

"Jurors whose names begin with "A" through "N" go to courtroom "A"," he instructed, and "O" through "Z" go to courtroom "B".'

Moon thought hard. Boone begins with a "B" and Moon begins with an "M". Should he follow the group into the first courtroom or should he go with the others to the second? It was then Lulabelle came to his rescue. She knew that Moon was no Einstein. She approached him and whispered into his ear, "Courtroom 'A'". Lulabelle and Mr. Bib Overalls followed the herd to Courtroom "B". He had no choice but to join the other group of jurors to Courtroom "A".

The courtroom was different from the jury room. There an elevated bench with a huge high backed chair behind it. The bench was flanked by two chairs surrounded by low fences in front. There was a small desk in front of the bench. To the right of the bench there were two rows of six chairs also behind a short fence. Moon and the other twenty-three prospective jurors were directed to be seated in a group in the courtroom which was also separated from the bench area by yet another short fence.

After a few short moments, the bailiff shouted, "All rise." The loud tone of the bailiff caused Moon to jump out of his seat. A tall man with a mane of white hair wearing a black robe entered into the courtroom from a door behind the bench which Moon had not noticed before.

Moon stood motionless while the man in the black robe seated himself behind the elevated bench.

After he was seated the bailiff, again in a loud voice, announced, "Hear ye, Hear ye, the Circuit Court of Union County, Arkansas, with the Honorable P. Nobel Peabody presiding, is now in session. All having business before the Court draw nigh and you will be heard. God save these United States and this Honorable Court."

"You may be seated," Judge Peabody told them. Moon, deeply impressed with the ceremony thus far, sank gratefully into his seat.

"I am Judge Peabody," the man in the black robe told them. "Seated to my left is Sadi McGillis, Clerk of this Court." Sadi dutifully rose and nodded politely to the panel.

The Judge went on, "To my right is the witness box where the persons who testify will be seated. In front of me is Charlotte Walker, who is the court reporter. She will take down every word that is said by repeating into the stenomask and later transcribe it."

Since Charlotte's face was covered with a mask-like contraption, she simply raised one hand to acknowledge she had heard all that had transpired. Moon, ever the gentleman, waved back at her.

Judge Peabody frowned at him. Moon hunkered in his seat. He was baffled by the stenomask. Was she breathing oxygen? Did she have a serious health problem? Moon wished he could see her face.

"Further to my right is the jury box," he told them. "Twelve persons from among you will be selected to hear the evidence presented, my instructions as to the law and then render a verdict either for or against the plaintiff."

"Since you are a new panel it is necessary that I empanel you. I will do so by asking some questions which will affect your qualifications to serve on this panel," he instructed them.

"First, are each of you citizens of the United States of America?"

No one denied citizenship and so he proceeded.

"Are you a registered voter in Union County, Arkansas?"

Moon felt a surge of pride. Ever since his mother had taken to register as a voter he had cast his ballot in every election. Again no one denied being a registered voter.

"Do each of you read and write the English language?"

This question caused Moon some consternation. It is true he did read and write. However, his academic skills were very limited. Nonetheless he reasoned that since the Judge did not ask how well he reads and writes he was safe in keeping his mouth shut.

"Have you ever been convicted of a felony?"

One hand went up. Judge Peabody asked, "What is your name?"

"Homer Hayes," the man replied.

"Have you been pardoned," asked the Judge.

"No, sir," responded Homer.

"Very well," said Judge Peabody, I have no alternative but to excuse you from this panel. You may leave. It is not necessary that you return."

"Are there any of you who are not physically able to serve?"

Three hands went up. One had a bad back that was aggravated by sitting. She was excused. Another had a kidney condition which prompted frequent trips to the rest room. He too was excused.

The third was a large, robust woman with a red face. She told Judge Peabody, "Ah gatta tend to my sick mama."

"What's the problem?" Judge Peabody inquired.

"Ain't nuthin' wrong with me. It's my mama who needs help," she told him.

Judge Peabody cleared his throat. "I understand that your mother needs help. What's wrong with your mother?"

"She done had a stroke," she told him

"Can't your father take care of her?" the Judge asked.

"He run off when I wuz six," she responded.

"Is she paralyzed?" the Judge wanted to know.

"She can't even pee lessen I help her to the toilet."

"You're excused," Judge Peabody told her.

Judge Peabody continued. "Are any of you doctors, nurses or other medical practitioner?"

No answers.

Evidently satisfied, Judge Peabody told them this was a civil case involving a motor vehicle accident that happened eighteen months before. Why judges and lawyers use the term "motor vehicle" rather than car or automobile or truck is an enigma which leaves a lay person shaking his or her head in bewilderment. Judge Peabody then told him that the plaintiff was William "Jack" Dempsey of El Dorado and the defendant was Lucy May Gilmore of Smackover. After Dempsey sued Ms. Gilmore she counterclaimed against him.

"Do any of you know either Mr. Dempsey or Ms. Gilmore?" Judge Peabody asked.

No one admitted to being acquainted with either.

"The accident happened on July 4th of last year, at the intersection of Faulkner and Main Streets in El Dorado," Judge Peabody informed them. "Do any of you have any information whatsoever regarding the accident?"

No answers.

"Do any of you expect to be called as a witness in this case?"

Again no answers.

"The lawyers in this case are F. Wilton Doster for the plaintiff and Thomas J. Freeman for the defendant," Judge Peabody advised. Do you know either of them or do either currently represent you?"

No one admitted to knowing or ever having been by either of represented by them.

"Very well," said Judge Peabody, "Do either of the lawyers have any questions?"

A tall slender man with horn rimmed glasses whose Adam's apple bobbed up and down like a cork on a fishing line arose.

"I am F. Wilton Doster," he commenced, "and I represent the plaintiff, Jack Dempsey."

He went on, "Have you read anything about the accident in the newspaper?"

Since the accident was only a fender bender Judge Peabody knew it was not written up in the local newspaper. Judge Peabody scowled at the lawyer.

"Are any of you of the opinion that one person should not sue another under any circumstance?"

There was no response.

"Have any of you had back trouble?"

So many hands went up that F. Wilton decided not to pursue that line of questioning any further.

"Have any of you ever been a plaintiff or a defendant in a lawsuit?"

Having had no positive responses, Doster went on, "I advertise on the radio. Would this cause any of you to be prejudiced against me?"

Before any of the jurors could respond the judge told the lawyer, "Sit down, Mr. Doster, I have heard enough."

"But your honor," protested F. Wilton.

"I said sit down, Mr Doster," Judge Peabody barked.

Doster sat.

Thomas J. Freeman, wearing a seersucker suit with a black string tie arose and bowed slightly. He squinted at the jurors for a long moment and said, "I'd be pleased for any member of this panel to serve. They are obviously good Arkansans who treasure the American way, truth and justice for all."

Judge Peabody looked as if he had bitten into a green persimmon. He then excused the jury for a fifteen minute break so as to allow the clerk to draw names from a cigar box.

While the jury was in recess, Ms. McGillis, Clerk of Court, drew 18 names from the cigar box, calling forth each name as it was drawn. Moon's name was the sixth drawn from the box.

When the jury panel returned to the courtroom Judge Peabody told them, "Ms. McGillis will call 18 of you to stand and be sworn. If your name is not called you are excused. I am uncertain when the next trial will be. The sheriff will notify you when to be present here again."

Sadi then called the 18 names of the jurors from the panel who had been drawn from the cigar box. When he heard his name Moon almost wet himself. This was a historic moment in his life. He shuffled with the other 17 to the front of the bench. Ms. McGillis told them to raise their right hands so as to take an oath. Since both of Moon's arms were hidden from his view by both his shirt and his coat, it made it impossible to see which arm bore his vaccination scar. His mother had taught him that he had been vaccinated on his left arm. He broke into a cold sweat. The other jurors raised their hands but Moon was so distraught that he was unable to translate from their raised hands to determine which was his right. In a tizzy, he raised his left arm above his head.

"You there," Judge Peabody said, "raise your other hand."

Moon obediently raised his right arm but neglected to lower his left arm. He appeared to be a man surrendering.

"Put your left arm down," Judge Peabody commanded.

Moon's face glowed as red as a baboon's behind. He lowered his right arm.

"Come forward," the Judge commanded.

Moon approached the bench with his left arm still raised high above his head.

"Put your arm down," Judge Peabody thundered.

Moon did so. He reached the front of the bench with his knees shaking so hand that he could barely stand. This was worse than the wild ride to the courthouse. It was even worse than flying through the woods on a four wheeler driven by his cousin Sweetpea Jeter. It was as bad as his taxi ride from the airport to his hotel in New York.

"What is your name?"

Moon could hardly speak. However, after biting his lower lip so hard that it almost drew blood, he was able to identify himself.

"You don't know your left from your right, do you?," asked Judge Peabody in a kinder, gentler voice.

"Not with a coat on," Moon answered.

"Would you like to be excused from jury duty, son?."

Moon swallowed hard. If being on a jury carried such grave responsibilities as knowing your left arm from your right with your vaccination scar hidden, then it would seem to him that other problems, even more perplexing could arise.

"Yes, sir," Moon replied in a shaky voice.

"Very well," intoned Judge Peabody, "you are excused for the term."

Moon hesitated. "When should I be back?," he asked.

"Never," the Judge told him. "Leave the courtroom now."

As time went by Moon's recollections of being called for jury duty became fond memories. He formed close associations with F. Lee Bailey and Johnny Cochran. Judge Peabody called upon him for advise on touchy legal issues. He had added another notch on the handle of the six gun of his achievements.

MOON AT THE FARM

Moon's mother was a Jeter before she married. The Jeters were a large, dysfunctional family who lived in a rickety old farm house sitting on a 60-acre tract in southwestern Union County. Her brother, Homer Jeter, known fondly by all as Possum, was a fat, hairy man of around sixty years. He always wore bib overalls and chewed Red Man tobacco. His red hair was thinning and one of his pale blue eyes was so crossed he could see only the bridge of his nose. He shaved every Saturday and consequently his florid cheeks were covered with a bristly red stubble for six days of the week.

The home place was built by Moon's grandfather when he returned home from the Spanish American War. It was an ugly house when it was built and the passing of the years had done nothing to improve it. It had last been painted forty years before and was covered with a faint hint of peeling yellow paint. It was occupied by Possum, his wife, Layde Ruth, his widowed sister, Homerette, his spinster sister, Rose of Sharon, and Possum's three sons. Two of his sons, Homer Lee and Homer Ray, worked occasionally at the gin close by Homer, Louisiana. Since the gin was in operation only during the three months of cotton picking, the Homers were at the home place most of the time. They spent their time tending to the family business, hunting, fishing and pursuing the local females. Their younger brother Homer Lynn, known affectionaly as Sweetpea, was recently paroled from the Arkansas prison at Cummins after spending a year as an inmate, having pled guilty to a charge of driving while intoxicated, fourth offense, and was home again.

Possum had an affinity for felines and owned probably a dozen or more cats of all species and genders. The cats were also residents of the household. Since they had never been housebroken the Jeter home was referred to by their neighbors as "Cat Piss Manor."

The Jeter farm was no more than fallow acreage. Other than the herd of cats who occupied the household and the wild animals which abounded, there were no cattle, swine or other livestock on the property. The antique chicken house no longer housed chickens. The roof of the old barn had caved in and provided a haven for a flock of bats. The property was so barren that it was avoided even by crows.

The pride of the Jeter estate was a huge copper pot, yards of copper tubing and a number two wash tub which was used to catch the steady flow of moonshine which poured in a never ending stream from the tubing. Possum was proud of his operation. Since he was not bent to farming, or anything else of a strenuous nature, all of the corn used in his operation was purchased from neighbors.

This was the family business. Possum and his offspring dipped the white lightening from the wash tub and funneled it into gallon jugs. Until he was incarcerated Sweeetpea delivered the product from the family still to thirsty customers in a tri-county area. He owned a 1950 Lincoln Towncar whose engine had been modified by installing overhead cams, oversized pistons and a fuel injection system. It could reach speeds to up to 120 miles per hour. Sweetpea was never caught and arrested for transporting moonshine but he had a drawer full of speeding tickets. Had it not been for his habit of drinking and driving he would have escaped incarceration altogether.

He spent the first week after his parole tuning and retuning his Lincoln which he fondly called the Silver Bullet. In and around Union County Sweetpea was a folk hero. He was tall, over six feet, and as lean as a stringbean. His slicked down black hair was resplendent, coated with Vaseline and highlighted by monstrous sideburns. Tattoos with such noble sayings as *Death before Dishonor* and *Mother* graced both arms. He always wore alligator boots with silver inlaid toes. He was desired by almost all of the girls and envied by all of the men in south Arkansas.

The local youths had composed a folk song in his honor which they would sing as Sweetpea sped by in this souped up Lincoln.

"See the Silver Bullet whizzin' by,
Sweetpea's got the hammer down,
If whiskey don't still him and speed don't kill him,

He'll make it through another round."

To understand the success of the Jeter family business you must understand the psyche of Union County, Arkansas. In those days, Union County was a dry county. That is to say, the sale of any alcoholic beverage, legally or illegally distilled, was prohibited by law. For over fifty years the law enforcement officers of the county had recognized the need for a buckler now and then and consequently accepted gratuities from likes of the Jeter family to insure a happy relationship between law enforcement and citizens of the county. Federal agents were so intimidated by the moonshiners that they stayed out of Union County.

Moon's mother was the only member of the Jeter family who disdained strong drink. As a result Moon was a teetotaler. Although forbidden by his mother to visit the Jeter estate, because of his friendship with his cousin, Sweetpea, Moon was a frequent visitor.

One bright spring day when he was fifteen Moon paid a visit to the Jeter family. Homer Ray had killed a wild hog that morning and the family had set about scalding and gutting the giant beast. A very large iron pot had a fire built under it and the water in it was boiling. The hog was lowered into the steaming contents of the pot and withdrawn after only a couple of minutes. The body of the swine was then scraped with an extremely sharp knife (the same knife that Possum used to cut chaws from a plug of Red Man) and then butchered.

All was proceeding as nicely as a hog butchering can be until three armed men, carrying 30.30 rifles with side arms strapped to their hips interrupted the family gathering. The big, ugly man wearing a badge, Moon learned later, was Sheriff Maynard T. Grubbs. His blue-black hair was in disarray and he had a week's growth of black stubble on his cheeks and chins (he had two of them). He addressed Possum:

"You are under arrest for the manufacture and sale of untaxed whiskey."

"Shucks, May," said Possum, "can't you take Sweetpea with you and leave us here to finish with this hawg."

"Is he authorized?" asked Maynard.

"Shore,'" Possum answered.

Maynard regarded Sweetpea with an icy stare. He told him, "You meet me at the sheriff's office in twenty minutes."

Sweetpea nodded and motioned for Moon to follow him into the house. He took a small leather bag from underneath a mattress in Possum's bedroom. Looking directly at Moon he told him, "Come on, Moon, were off the see the sheriff."

Moon's entire body was quivering like a bowl of jelly. Nonetheless he followed his cousin to the Silver Bullet to commence the short trip to the office of the Sheriff of Union County, Arkansas, convinced that he would be arrested, strip searched and imprisoned for the rest of his life.

The office of the sheriff provided not only a gathering place for the sheriff and his deputies but also furnished accommodations for guests of the county at the jail in the rear of the sheriff's digs. The jail was dark, dank and foul smelling. There is something unique about southern jails. There is a rich aroma of tobacco smoke, urine and unwashed bodies. There was no air conditioning and the hot dusty air was hard to breath. No fans circulated the foul air, and the prisoners lounged about in their underwear.

The office of Sheriff Grubbs was a room approximately 12 feet by 12 feet. It consisted of a large wood desk that was probably fairly new when the Confederates fired upon Fort Sumpter. A large desk chair behind the desk accommodated the bulky body of the sheriff. Two brown folding chairs in front of the desk completed the drab furnishing. There was a large gun rack on one wall housing both rifles and shotguns. The other wall had a wooden plaque on it.

When Moon entered into the office his rotund body was shaking more than ever. The sheriff was not there when he and Sweetpea entered so Moon examined the plaque. There was a section of rubber hose attached to it and underneath there was the simple inscription "Lie Detector." Moon's knees grew so unsteady that he sat down in one of the rickety chairs.

Sweetpea lounged in the other chair. When Sheriff Grubbs entered the room Moon wet his pants. At age fifteen his life was over.

The sheriff sat down and Sweetpea passed him the small leather bag. Sheriff Grubbs peered into the bag and appeared to be counting something. When his counting was done he told them, "Okay, boys, you can leave."

Moon was speechless. It was as if the governor had handed him a pardon for his offences. Shaking his wet leg Moon departed the premises. Moon's one and only brush with the law ended on a high note.

STONEWALL JACKSON BOONE, U.S.M.C.

Moon reached his sixteenth birthday on November 15, 1950. Although reading and interpreting a newspaper was somewhat over his head, he knew from listening to his Philco radio which was a gift from his mother, that the Seventh Marine Regiment had crossed the 38th parallel in Korea where they encountered a massive counterattack from the army of China. The Chinese army met the Seventh Marine Regiment at the Chosen Reservoir in late November of 1950, where a bloody battle lasted for six days. One of the bravest chapters in the annals of warfare was written with a quill dipped in the blood of the Seventh Marine Regiment.

His uncle, Homer Jeter, was a veteran of World War II. Homer could have been a good enough soldier had he concentrated on military duties. However, he and one Willie Puckett from Tunica, Mississippi, tore some of the copper tubing from a latrine while in basic training and used it to construct a crude still which, from apple cores, potato peels, corn cobs and the like, produced a clear liquid which Willie and Homer dubbed "apple jack". They consumed so much of the first batch that they developed severe stomach cramps and were hospitalized. When their moonshining activities came to light they were court-martialed. Homer was sentenced to six months in the stockade for destroying government property and another six months for being intoxicated while on duty. When Homer was released from confinement the war was over and he received a dishonorable discharge. His only complaint about his military service was that he did not receive a Purple Heart on account of his stomach cramps.

Moon's father was also a soldier who spent the war breaking horses at Fort Hood, Texas, for the First Calvary. He received an Honorable Discharge.

While passing by a Marine Recruiting Office one bright winter day, Moon was called inside by a tall man in a dress blues uniform. He wore corporal stripes on his arms and his chest was covered with bright colored ribbons. The Marine's dark blue trousers had a red stripe and he wore white gloves. The gold buttons on his blue tunic were polished to a high sheen, and his shoes were spit shined so brightly that they reflected the overhead light fixture. Moon had never seen anything so splendid.

He asked Moon, "How would you like to serve your country in her hour of need?"

"Sure", said Moon, "But how?"

"By joinin' the Corps," the young corporal said with a very serious look. "How old are you?"

Moon was uncertain as to what to say. "How old do I have to be?"

"Eighteen," he was told.

"Then I'm eighteen," Moon told him. Moon was having a grand time although he knew his wish to be a Marine would never be granted.

"When were you born?," asked the Marine whom Moon believed to be at least a general.

"1934," Moon proudly told him.

The Marine frowned. "Don't you mean 1932?"

Moon had never been good at dates. "I guess so," he told the recruiter.

"I'll tell you what," the Corporal, whose name was Terry N. Traywick, told Moon, "you just sign this paper and we'll have you on a train for San Diego this afternoon. They'll be waitin' for you to fit you in your dress blues".

Moon pictured himself resplendent in a blue tunic with shiny buttons and blue pants with a red stripe.

"I'll sign," he said.

"Now, go home, pack a small bag and be back here in two hours," Corporal Tryawick told him. "Don't tell you folks what you have done so you can surprise them with a picture in your dress blues."

Moon didn't think it quite right to leave home without telling his mother. However, he reasoned that she would be very proud to see him in his dress blues, a proud member of the United States Marine Corps. So he did what he was told and packed a small bag. There wasn't room for his teddy bear, so he left him on his pillow.

"Don't worry, Yogi," he told the fuzzy doll, "I'll be back before long."

Moon returned to the recruiting office where he encountered Corporal Traywick. The corporal was delighted to see him.

"Just in time," Moon was told. "There's a chartered bus outside. Get on it. It will take you to the train station."

Moon boarded the bus and seated himself beside a strange looking guy who had orange hair cut like a rooster's comb.

The bus driver entered the bus and Moon left for his great adventure in a trail of exhaust fumes.

Mr. Orange Hair addressed Moon. "What's your handle, man?," he was asked.

"Don't have no handle," Moon told him.

"Your name, man, your name," Mr. Orange Hair told him.

Moon identified himself.

"Hey, Mooner," his new friend intoned. "How's it hangin'?"

Moon did not know what he was talking about so he simply grinned.

It was only a short trip to the train station where they were joined by five others who had been recruited by Corporal Traywick.

After sitting in the hot, dusty train station for over an hour, they were summoned by another Marine in stiff khakis.

"You lop-eared recruits get your fat butts on this train, on the double," the new Marine shouted.

Moon and the others stampeded into the train. It was obvious that this man meant business. The train blew its whistle and began to inch forward. Moon was beginning to doubt the wisdom of becoming a Marine. Although he had been gone from home less than three hours he felt a deep sense of regret. He missed his Moma and Yogi. He wondered if he would ever see them again.

It was a peaceful two-day train ride from El Dorado to San Diego. They arrived at Marine Corps Recruit Depot at San Diego at 1300 hours (Moon was never able to master the military method for telling time). Upon their arrival the tranquility they had enjoyed during the train trip was broken by their new drill instructor, Sergeant Moses Burks. He wore stiff fatigues and a felt hat blocked to a peak with a gold globe and anchor on the front. Sergeant Burks greeted them in a very loud voice as follows:

"You lop-eared mangy peckerwoods will become Marines even if it kills you. You will be on duty twenty hours a day. You will sleep when I tell you to sleep. You will shower and shave when I tell you. You will live for no purpose than becoming good Marines. Do you understand me?"

"Yes, sir," a few replied.

"I can't hear you," the sergeant shouted.

"Yes, sir," they all screamed.

"I still can't hear you."

"Yes, sir," they responded with a roar.

"I am Staff Sergeant Moses Burks," he told them. "Before you leave here you will hate me worse than the devil hates holy water. You will eat, sleep and dream of nothing but the United States Marine Corps. Do you follow me?".

"Yes, sir," they loudly responded.

"Now, line up according to height," the group was told.

Since Moon stood only 5'2" it was easy for him to find his position at the foot of the line of new recruits.

"March, you dumb rednecks," Sergeant Burks told them.

They began to march.

"Halt, you morons," the good sergeant shouted. "You began with your left foot."

This became a source of deep consternation for Moon. He could not discern his left from his right unless he could see his vaccination scar on his left arm. He cut his eyes to his right to see which foot his neighbor put first.

"You there, dummy," Sergeant Burks addressed Moon, "You keep your eyes straight ahead. Don't look to see what the knothead next to you is doin.'"

Moon turned his head to face straight ahead so swiftly that it caused a crick in his neck.

"Forward march," they were ordered.

Moon stepped forward on his right foot.

Sergeant Burks drew a deep breath and commenced to count cadence.

"I don't know, but I been told that Eskimo women are mighty cold," chanted Sergeant Burks, as they followed him. "Sound off". "One, two," they all counted. "Sound off." Sergeant Burks repeated. "Three, four," they all responded. "Left, right, left," he repeated over and over.

They marched to a large wooden building. Inside were four barber chairs, and behind each chair was a grinning barber armed with clippers.

Four at a time they were seated in the chairs. Each haircut took approximately thirty seconds. As each recruit arose from the barber's chair he was bald as a newborn baby.

Mr. Orange Hair, whose real name was Oscar Jerome Pride, sat in the chair. He told the barber, "light neck trim, leave the sideburns bushy." A half of minute later he too was as bald as a cue ball.

Moon sadly watched his black curls disappear under the steady hum of the clippers. The floor was covered with black, brown, blond and, yes, even orange hair. Moon sighed deeply.

They were then herded to the back of the barracks where they lined up single file in front of a long counter manned by two growling sergeants.

"Give me your shoe size, and pass down the line," they were told.

The first thing they were given was a tin bucket. As the moved down the line at the counter they were supplied with fatigues, brogans, wool socks, underwear, shapeless caps and green T-shirts all of which were deposited in their buckets. Moon wondered about his dress blues but decided this was not the best time to ask.

They were then marched to a concrete block building called the armory. Each was handed an M-l rifle.

"The rifle is your best friend," Sergeant Burks told them. "Treat her like she is your sweetheart. If I even hear of any one of you maggots abusing her, you will answer to me. Do you understand me?"

"Yes, sir," they shouted in unison. They were catching on fast.

"This is a U.S. Rifle Caliber 30, M-1. It is the finest piece of fighting equipment ever made. When you get to Korea it will save your life. Do you understand me?

Another loud course of "yes, sirs" was heard.

"Always remember, this is not a gun. It is a rifle. If I hear any one of you peaheads call it a gun, I'll make you regret it. Do you understand me?"

"Yes, sir," they all shouted.

"You are assigned to Barracks 'A'," he told them. "You got thirty minutes to pack your civies, change into fatigues and brogans and make up your bunks. Now, git!"

They hurried like they had never hurried before. All were dressed in fatigues and boots within the allotted time. Moon's pants were six inches too long. He had rolled them up as best he could. Because of his tremendous girth he was unable to button the jacket of his fatigues. He looked like a refugee from a Good Will store. Moon was beginning to have serious doubts about the wisdom of enlisting.

When they reassembled on the parade grounds, they again lined up according to height. Moon breathed a sight of relief secure in the knowledge that because of his statute he would be the last in line.

One of the new skinheads, whom Moon subsequently learned was Elvis Presley McDonald, complained to Sergeant Burks that his stomach was hurting and that he need to go to a doctor. The good sergeant told him: "There was a recruit in the last bunch that came through here who complained of stomach cramps the first day. I sent him to sick bay. The doc couldn't find nuthin wrong with him. The next day he complained against and I send him back to sick bay with a suggestion to the doc. The doc liked my suggestion and he told the peckerwood that he had found what his trouble was so he circumcised him. He never asked to go to sick bay again. Now, numbskull, do you still want to go to sick bay?"

Elvis swallowed hard and said in a trembling voice, "No, sir, I feel much better now".

Sergeant Burks addressed the platoon loudly: "Even you knuckleheads got to eat. Off to the mess hall. Right face."

All turned right except Moon who turned to his left. Sergeant Burks' face turned beet red. He squinted at Moon, who was almost trembling.

All of his life Moon had been unable to tell his left from his right unless he could see his vaccination scar on his left arm.

"You skinheaded snot sucking moron," Sergeant Burks commenced. "First you started close order drill on the wrong foot and now you can't make a right face. What the hell is wrong with you?"

"I guess I need more practice," Moon replied in a shaky voice.

Sergeant Burks glowered. Nevertheless, since they were almost late for their dinner, so he told them again:

"Right face".

The sergeant sighed deeply when Moon turned first to his left, but then corrected himself by turning right.

"Forward march," an exasperated Sergeant Burks commanded.

His consternation deepened as he watched Moon start forward with his right foot.

In the mess hall they followed one another down in a line in front of steaming pots of food. Behind each pot was a man in a green undershirt holding a large spoon in his hand. Each recruit had a tray and an oval shaped plate. As the passed down the line giant helpings of the contents of the pots were splashed onto their trays. When they reached the end of the line they moved to long wooden tables where they commenced to devour the contents of their trays.

"All right, ladies," Sergeant Burks spoke in a loud voice, "put your leftovers in the barrel by the door and then go to the barracks and get your rifles. You got ten minutes to assemble on the parade grounds."

Thirty new recruits fell over one another scraping scraps of their meal into the large barrel and then running to their barracks. All assembled on the parade grounds carrying their rifles.

"What's that thing in your hand," Sergeant Burls demanded of Moon.

In a trembling voice Moon told him, "It's my gun, sir."

"You miserable moron," the good sergeant shouted, "didn't I tell you not to call it a gun? Now tell me what it is."

Moon was miserable. "It looks like a gun," he told him. "I don't know what else to call it."

"Unbutton you pants," Sergeant Burks to him.

This certainly seemed to be a strange request but nonetheless Moon did as he was told.

"Hold your rifle in one hand. Point to your unbuttoned pants with the other and repeat after me," Sergeant Burks told him. "This is my rifle and this is my gun. One is for war and one is for fun."

Moon was not good at poetry. "What did you want me to say," he asked in a trembling voice.

The good sergeant gave Moon a stern look. He asked, "How old are you?"

"Eighteen, sir," Moon stuttered.

"When were your born?"

Moon hesitated. He couldn't remember the year Corporal Traywick told him he had been born. He couldn't count backwards for eighteen years preceding 1950. He froze, unable to speak.

Sergeant Burks tried another tactic. "Son, what year were you born in?"

Moon bit his lip. This was it he thought. They would shackle him and lead him away to the brig. He wondered whether he would he face a firing squad.

He stammered, "1934, Sir."

"Do you know that makes you 16," Sergeant Burks asked.

"Yes, yes, sir," came Moon's shaky reply.

"Didn't the recruiting officer ask you your age?"

"I told him I was born in 1934, but he told me it was 1932. I didn't think to argue with him," Moon confessed.

"Do you want to go home," Sergeant Burks asked him.

"Yes, sir," Moon mumbled.

Sergeant Burks was visibly relieved.

"Go to the barracks, son," Sergeant Burks told him. "We'll do the paperwork to get you outta here tomorrow."

The good sergeant then addressed the other recruits, "All right you miserable pussy cats fall in for close order drill."

Moon did as directed and returned to the barracks. He had not had time to observe what was in there before and he set about inspecting it.

The barracks was old, wooden and dark. There were fifteen bunks covered with thin cotton mattresses on either side to the large room. Each bunk had a foot locker in front of it. There were hallways on each end of the building. There were two large rooms opening onto the hall at one end. One had a sign denoting it to be the supply room. The other had a sign saying *Drill Instructor, Keep Out.* The other hal way separated what Moon had always called a bathroom. The one on the right housed toilets and wash basins. The left had showers.

After his inspection of the barracks, Moon sat on an unmade bunk. He hoped he did not get Corporal Traywick in trouble. With visions of home, Momma, Pappy and Yogi dancing in his mind, Moon dropped off to sleep.

Shortly after he dozed off, his nap was interrupted by sounds of twenty nine sets of feet encased in heavy brogans racing across the wooden barracks floor. Each recruit stopped in front of a bunk and stood at rigid attention in front of it.

Sergeant Burks addressed them, "Well you morons have almost made it through your first day. Line up outside the supply room. You will get two sheets, a blanket, a pillow case and a pillow. You will return to your bunk and make it up. The blanket has gotta be stretched so tight that I can bounce a quarter off it. If none of you pussy cats can make a square corner on your bunk, you better get somebody to show you how. You got 15 minutes."

They all rushed to the supply room at the end of the barracks where they received the necessary supplies to make up a bed, military fashion. Moon was uncertain as to his role in the process so he stood last in line at the supply room where he was furnished with sheets and the like.

He found an empty bunk and made it up as best he could.

"Attention," someone shouted as Sergeant Burks strolled into the room. Each returned to his original position at the foot of his bunk. They stood with shoulders back, chest out, chin pressed to their respective necks. All stared straight ahead. They were catching on fast.

The sergeant walked past each bunk. On five of them he yanked back the blankets, sheets and mattresses and threw them on the floor. He looked at Moon's bunk, sighed deeply and moved on.

"If you ladies wanna get some shut-eye you best chip in and help your buddy make up his bunk. If anyone fails when I recheck you all will sleep on the floor," he told them.

"Do you understand me." he shouted.

"Yes, sir," they all shouted.

"I still can't hear you."

"Yes, sir," they screamed in unison.

"Then get your butts in gear," he commanded them.

Like a colony of fire ants they began picking up scattered mattresses, sheets and blankets and began remaking the beds.

Sergeant Burks walked around all of the bunks a second time.

"They's still a mess. I'm gonna let you sleep in them tonight, but tomorrow they better be tighter or you will not sleep at all," he told them.

Sergeant Burks went on, "It's 2100 hours. Lights out at 2200 hours. Reverie is at 0500 hours. You will make up your bunks, shower, shave and dress by 0530 hours 'cause that's when we will meet on the parade grounds. Do you understand me?"

They anticipated his question and shouted as one, "Yes, sir".

Moon sat on his bunk and stared at the scrubbed wooden floor. Things weren't working out. What would Sergeant Burks do with him in the morning? A new recruit approached him.

"I am J. Arthur Travis," he announced, "from Chicago." I am unable to comprehend Sergeant Burks' hostile treatment of us. What do you think?"

Moon stared at him as if he were from another planet.

"What's Chicago," he asked.

J. Arthur stared at him, sighed deeply and moved away, shaking his head.

Moon did not speak to anyone else that lonely night. However, he overheard from other conversations drifting around the barracks, that one young man was from a place called Possum Kingdom, in Arkansas. He was nicknamed "Gourd Head" that very evening.

Moon was awakened by an ear-splitting bugle call at an ungodly hour. The good sergeant walked the aisles which separated their bunks speaking harshly while admonishing them to get their sorry butts out of their nests. Moon dutifully rose from his bed and followed the others to what was called the "head". Sergeant Burks instructed them to shave, shower, make up their bunks and appear on the parade grounds in fifteen minutes for close order drill. Since Moon had no whiskers he escaped the shaving part.

Arriving at the parade grounds with his fly unbuttoned and his brogans untied, Moon was not the picture of a picture perfect Marine. His shirt was at least two sizes too small and his pants legs drug the ground.

Sergeant Burks addressed the group:

"You pussy cats stand at attention until I get back. If anybody moves, even to scratch his nose, I'll know about it and deal with him severely."

They snapped to, backs rigid and chins pressed against their chests.

He then took Moon by his arm and told him:

"Follow me."

They proceeded to a wooden building that look no different than the others at the recruit depot. Entering through the front door they were greeted by a grizzled veteran wearing corporal stripes sitting behind a scarred oak desk. The corporal was Edward Vaught, a twenty-year veteran of the Corps who had fought in both World War II and Korea. He had a drawer full of medals including three Purple Hearts. Corporal Vaught had been up and down the ranks so may times that the arms of his uniforms were threadbare. Were it not for strong drink he would still be a master sergeant. He looked at Moon and the sergeant with a critical eye.

"Gotta a baby blue Marine?" he asked.

"Yep. Gotta see the old man," Sergeant Burks replied. Burks had a great respect for Vaught. Being with the First Marine Regiment in the Pacific, Vaught was one of the first of the Americans to arrive in Korea. Although there only for two months he suffered three separate wounds. While in a hospital in Kobe, he sneaked out, got drunk and was AWOL for a week. When he returned to the hospital he was hung over, tired and hungry. He was broken from a master sergeant to a corporal and shipped back home. He accepted his punishment without a whimper, observing to his mates, "If I'd been workin' somewheres, they'da fired me."

He rose from his desk, knocked on the door in back of him, and entered into the next room. Minutes later, he exited through the same door and told them,

"The old man'll see ya now."

They entered into the room, which turned out to be the office of Second Lieutenant Roscoe Q. Lemon, the "old man." The old man appeared to be no older than twenty. Seated behind a somewhat newer and less scarred desk than the one assigned to Corporal Vaught, the Lieutenant had large brown eyes accented by large round spectacles. He had closely cut hair which must have been blond at one time, rosy red lips and a weak chin.

All of the Marines were bareheaded. Marines do not wear headgear indoors, and since they are uncovered, they do not salute.

"What's your business, sergeant?" Lieutenant Lemon asked.

"We got ourselves a tadpole, sir," answered Sergeant Burks.

Lieutenant Lemon squinted and asked Moon, "How old are you, son?"

Moon bit his lower lip. "S-s-sixteen", Moon stammered.

"Whatever made you join the Corps?"

Moon rolled his eyes. "I don't know."

Lieutenant Lemon summoned Corporal Vaught.

"Corporal," Lieutenant Lemon instructed, "process this man for immediate separation from the Corps, and I mean right now."

"Aye, sir," Corporal Vaught answered.

And, sure enough, after a maze of paperwork, Moon dressed himself in his civilian clothes and was escorted off the base in a jeep driven by a Marine who surely must have been a relative of Barney Oldfield. He had one day's pay, $10.00 and a General Discharge Under Honorable Conditions.

The rest of the story played out as you may have suspected. Moon's mother had plagued the entire Pentagon, all of the Arkansas delegation in Congress, and the office of the President himself. Had she not learned that her baby was on the way home she would have struck off for California in the family's old Nash Rambler.

When Moon arrived home his mother was waiting with outstretched arms. The prodigal son had come home. She scolded him severely then took him into their house and fed him animal crackers and pink lemonade. Moon stuck his teddy bear under his arm while nibbling his animal crackers and sipping his lemonade. He sighed deeply. It was good to be home.

MOON AND THE SNAKE OIL MAN

Amelia Boone, Moon's older sister, was regarded in her neighborhood as strange. As contrasted to Moon's height of five feet two inches, Amanda stood six feet one inch in her stocking feet. When she enrolled as a sophomore at El Dorado High she immediately caught the eye of the girl's basketball coach Dudley Thomas. Following a period of coaxing by Coach Thomas, Amelia joined the team. After two of the most frustrating weeks of his life, it became apparent to Coach Thomas that Amanda's limited attention span prevented her from learning the finer parts of the game, such as to which end of the court she should try to score. Amelia took her ouster from the team with a sign of relief. No longer would her afternoons be filled with running up and down the court bouncing a large ball. But rather she could fulfill her life's ambition of selling used hammers. While not possessing the most outstanding learning ability, it appeared that Amanda would be the first Boone ever to graduate from high school. What she lacked in intellect, she made up in hard work. She became a great source of pride to her parents who started a modest savings plan so, if God were to be willing, she could attend, of all things, college.

At an early age, Amelia acquired an unusual avocation. She collected used hammers. When her collection grew to include sledge hammers, ball peen hammers, claw hammers, tack hammers, and all sorts of other hammers, Amanda decided to embark into the complex world of business. A large wooden tray was acquired. Using one of her hammers, Amelia nailed leather thongs to either end of the tray. She then put the thong around her neck, filled her tray with a collection of hammers and commenced to call upon her neighbors, one by one, soliciting the sale of hammers.

Unfortunately, the market for used hammers was slow. Indeed, it was nonexistant. Despite her dogged determination to corner the used hammer market in El Dorado, Amelia failed to make a single sale although Tiny Tim Tolliver agreed to buy one if he could raise a dollar. Evidently his efforts at raising money were as unsuccessful as Amelia's venture into the exciting world of used hammers because he never bought a hammer.

On the fourth day of soliciting, Amelia had scoured almost all of El Dorado. She set on a curb with her tray of hammers on her knees to relieve the pressure on her neck which was beginning to bend forward on account of the weight of a tray full of used hammers. While sitting on the curb contemplating the apparent failure of her first business venture, a strange thing happened. A shiny roadster pulled over to the curb and a gentleman resplendent in a snow white suit, black shirt, white tie and black and white wing tipped shoes sprang from the vehicle. He had long black hair tied in a pony tail and he was smoking a small cigar.

"And what, if I may ask, causes such a beautiful young damsel to be in such apparent distress," he asked in a rich bass voice.

"I been carryin' these hammers for four days and ain't sold a single one", she told him.

"You're peddling the wrong product, my dear", the stranger told her. "I am Franklin D. Roosevelt Jones but you may call me Mr. Jones," he told her. "I am the president and CEO of Jones Enterprises, the largest distributor in the nation. Come to work for me and I will make you rich."

Amelia didn't notice that he did not say what he distributed. But somehow what he had told her didn't compute. What would she have to do to get rich? How much money is "rich"? Could she remain in El Dorado? Could she continue to pursue her high school diploma?

She squinted at her prospective employer. "What's the deal?" she asked.

"Car washes," he replied.

Amelia was skeptical. "There's whole heap of car washes in El Dorado," she observed.

"Ah, yes," he told her. "You are astute beyond your years. But I, the greatest distributor in the world, will put them all out of business."

She didn't speak, but rather looked at him with quizzical eyes. He went on, "You see, my dear, my car washes will be staffed with women."

Amelia was perplexed. "Why will folks come to have their cars git washed by women?" she asked.

"Because, my women will be topless." He told her in a triumphal voice that sounded as if he had just discovered the lost ark.

She was shocked beyond words. "You mean, they will take their shirts off?"

"Not only their shirts, but also their undergarments as well. I have already enlisted the services of Daisy from Maxine's House of Joy," he told her with smug satisfaction.

"No, sirree bob," she told him in no uncertain terms. "My mama told me never to do that kinda stuff."

She picked up her tray and started to put it around her neck.

"But wait," Franklin D. Roosevelt Jones said to her. "If you disdain appearing topless, nonetheless there are investment opportunities. I will guarantee to triple your investment in my company within sixty days."

"Ain't got no money," she told him.

"What about your family, are there any businessmen related to you?"

"Sure are," she proudly told him. "My brother Moon is the best businessman in El Dorado."

"And where can I find this gentleman," he asked her.

"Fred's Pool hall I recko," came her prompt reply.

"I, too, am an accomplished billiard player," he told her. "How do I get to Fred's?"

Amelia gave him careful directions on how to get to Fred's.

"Alas, my fair one, while I am disappointed you have turned down my offer to employ you at one of my car washes, I am impressed with your virtue. May the soft rains fall gently on your back and your trip through life be blessed. Vaya con Dios, mi dulce."

She looked at as if he had just swallowed a frog.

Mr. Jones jumped into his roadster and left Amelia in a cloud of exhaust smoke, on a mission to snare her rich brother into the topless car wash business.

Arriving at Fred's, Mr. Jones entered into the smoky, dimly lit interior. When his eyes adjusted to the semi-darkness, he observed five pool tables, all in use by men who ranged in age 16 to 75. He asked Otis, the rack boy, to identify Moon Boone. Otis pointed out Moon, seated in a high backed chair watching the pool sharks at works.

When Mr. Jones started across the room toward Moon, Moon became instantly alert. Here, he thought, is a prospective shoe customer. The stranger could be good for two or three pair, or maybe even more if Moon used all of his persuasive tactics—such a persistent attack until his new customer wilts under endless assertions and promises. Moon pushed his sample case forward and fingered his order pad.

When Mr. Jones arrived at Moon's chair he stuck out his hand and grasped Moon's outstretched hand with such force that Moon heard his knuckles crack. He introduced himself and began his spiel before Moon could catch his breath. This was most unusual. Most of his customers avoided him like the plague, making it necessary for Moon to hunt them down and remove their shoes while they were in a moment of quite repose. Moon looked at the stranger's feet which were shod in black and white wing tips. Moon knew instantly that this would be a hard sale because the stranger obviously had impeccable taste. So engrossed was Moon in sizing up this prospective customer that the words pouring forth from the stranger went unnoticed. Then Moon heard the word "topless". This caught his attention.

"Why would folks want their cars washed by a bunch of guys with their shirts off?" Moon asked.

"Not guys, Mr. Boone, but beautiful young women with full figures."

Moon was shocked beyond words. "Why did you come to see me?" he demanded to know.

"Because your lovely sister suggested that I talk with you."

And then and there, Moon Boone, who had never even talked harshly to another person, let alone struck one, reacted to the stranger's remark about Amelia by coming off of his high backed chair and swinging his fist into the belly of Franklin D. Roosevelt Jones. Moon hit him in the stomach because he was too short to reach his chin. Every one of the pool players at Fred's stopped their respective games and stared with eyes and mouths agape. Mr. Jones, when he recovered his breath, drew back his fist to strike Moon. This immediately triggered a response from the patrons of the pool hall. Otis reached the stranger first and grabbed his arm so as to prevent him from striking Moon. The others arrived seconds later. Together they dumped Franklin D. Roosevelt Jones onto the sidewalk in front of Fred's, causing his white suit to be the worse for wear.

"And don't you never come back here, you low lifed polecat," Otis admonished him. "If'n you do, we'll string you up."

Franklin D. Roosevelt Jones ran, not walked, to his roadster and sped away, leaving Fred's and the rest of El Dorado as far behind him as he could.

The patrons of Fred's crowded around Moon. They toasted him with Miller High Life while Moon, happy as a hog in the sunshine, contentedly sipped on a coke.

The crowd was so responsive to Moon's protection for his sister that six of them bought new shoes even though they still had the last ones Moon sold them in the unopened boxes. It was a grand day for Moon Boone, hero of the hour.

MOON AND THE LOVE BUG

When Moon was at West Side Baptist School he became smitten with Miss Suzie Slagle, his blonde and shapely teacher in the second grade. He washed blackboards, emptied trash barrels, and performed every menial task imaginable without even being asked. Had she asked him to ski down the slope of Joe T. Robinson mountain he would have tried although there had never been a flake of snow on the mountain. Indeed, Ms. Slagle became so distraught by his obvious attention that she promoted him to the third grade after a tenure of only one year in the second. After his year with Ms. Slagle, Moon did not become aware of the opposite sex, other than the employees of the house of joy over the pool hall, until he met Ms. Maybelle McGinnis.

Maybelle was not the picture of a beauty queen. She, like Moon, was short and stout. Her dingy blonde hair hung loosely over her large shoulders and she chewed gum at a rate of six packs a day. She worked in ticket sales at the Rialto Theater, sitting in a lonely booth, distributing tickets and taking cash from moviegoers. Since Moon was at the Rialto every time the picture changed, he would purchase a ticket from her every week or so. They became speaking acquaintances, chatting about such things as the weather and current events. Moon, being totally aware of current events, would listen intently listen to what she said and gravely nod his head in silent assent.

Then one day an astonishing thing happened. While chatting happily about the increased cost of popcorn, Maybelle shyly asked Moon whether he would meet her for coffee after the ticket office closed. Moon blinked his eyes and felt a pounding in his chest. Was this goddess actually asking him for a date? What should he do? Should he tell her that he didn't drink coffee?

Finally, after recovering his breath, he asked her, "Where?"

"At the soda fountain of Izzy's Drug Store. They stay open until eleven. Let's meet at ten-thirty when I get off."

"Okay", Moon stammered before he rushed in side the theater to watch John Wayne defeat rustlers, Nazis, the Viet Cong, or whomsoever else might appear.

Inside the theater the silver screen lighted but Moon was in such a state that he could not concentrate on his hero besting bad guys of all nationalities and colors. He decided that he could drink a coke by explaining that coffee (which he had never tasted) would not allow him to sleep.

He could not figure out what to talk about other then the weather. Then he hit on a solution. He would seek the advise of Otis at the pool hall. Otis was a man of the world and would understand matters of the heart.

Moon bolted from the theater and rushed to the pool hall where he found Otis cleaning spittoons with a rag that looked like it could stand on its own without folding. Otis was as tall as Moon was short. He had unkempt blonde hair that reminded one of the scarecrow in the Wizard of Oz. There was the familiar chaw of tobacco in his cheek, and his protruding Adam's apple bobbed up and down like a raft shooting the rapids on an untamed river. Moon explained his dilemma. Otis gravely stared at Moon.

"Okay," Otis told him, "the first thing that you gotta do is carry her flowers."

"Where would I get flowers this late at night? And, besides all the money I had was to buy popcorn with," Moon replied, realizing in his rush to be counseled by Otis he forgot to buy his usual huge box of buttered popcorn.

Otis had a simple explanation. "They buried the widder Westmoreland today. There waz lots of flowers on her grave. Go help yourself."

"Won't she care?" inquired an anxious Moon.

"Hell no," Otis answered. "She done died and don't care a hoot 'bout flowers. And 'sides that they won't cost you a cent."

Otis' logic was irrefutable. Even so, there was something about Otis' logic that didn't seem quite right. However, Moon couldn't put his finger on it. He rationalized that Ms. Westmoreland wouldn't miss the flowers, and consequently Otis was, as usual, right.

"What can we talk about?" Moon inquired.

"Write her a pome," Otis suggested.

"Don't know how to write a pome," Moon responded.

"Hell, boy, I'll write one fer ya," Otis told him.

Before putting pen to paper, Otis gazed at Moon with a stern look in his eye.

"Go sit over yonder and don't make a peep till I'm done," Otis admonished.

Moon moved across the room and planted his round bottom on a high back chair used by observers of games of spirited nine ball, straights or eight ball and sat quietly watching Otis chew on a stub of a pencil staring at a blank piece of white paper.

After what seemed to be a protracted period of time, his muse, never far away, landed on Otis' shoulder and he commenced to write with a painstaking lack of speed.

When he finished he motioned for Moon to come read his masterpiece. Moon leapt from his chair and bounded across the room where Otis read to him the ode of affairs of the heart:

> Since the day that first I met you,
> You've been the one whom I adore,
> I loved you then, I'll love you when,
> Your tits hang down to the floor.

Upon hearing Otis' love poem Moon was breathless. Never before had he been exposed to such a grand literary work. He grabbed the scrap of paper declaring his undying love for the fair Maybelle from the grimy hand of Otis and began walking at a fast pace to the cemetery where the widow Westmoreland would rest for all eternity.

Arriving at the final resting place of Mrs. Westmoreland, Moon had no problem in locating her burial site as it was covered with bouquets of flowers. Moon grabbed a hand full of daisies and commenced to walk at an even faster pace to Izzy's Drug Store. Sure enough, sitting at the soda fountain sipping something from a cup was the fair Maybelle.

Breathless from so much activity, Moon slumped in the stool adjoining the stool where Maybelle perched.

"Maybelle," he panted, "I got you sumthin'." Whereupon he handed her the daisies, which had commenced to droop in silent protest from being yanked from the scene of the widder Westomoreland's place of interment.

"Why, Moon," Maybelle crooned, "How sweet. But how did you find flowers this time of night?"

Moon hesitated before answering. "Otis told me where to get 'em," Moon answered. He reasoned that telling the rest of the story may have caused Maybelle some consternation.

"And I wrote a pome for you," he told her. With trembling hand, he surrendered to poem to her.

Maybelle, pursing her lips together, commenced to read. After a few moments she spoke breathlessly, "Moon, this is the loveliest poem that I have ever read. Do you want to get married?"

Moon bit hard on the straw from which he was sipping cola. His mama would never permit him to wed. Besides, what would he do with a wife? He would be deprived of his nocturnal visits to Maxine's House of Joy. He could no longer linger in his bed until noon before starting another day in the shoe peddling business. He would be henpecked.

Moon turned crimson red. He leapt from his stool and departed Izzy's like a man being chased by a swarm of bees. Ever after, he would have Otis buy him a ticket to the Rialto so as not to be confronted by the fair Maybelle.

MOON AND BLACK GOLD

Moon's only interest in money was to have enough to reward one of the girls at Maxine's for a pleasant session. He lived for two things, selling shoes and visiting Maxine's young ladies.

One very hot August day, Moon was removing the shoes of a slight blonde man who had only three fingers on his right hand. He was sitting in a high back stool in Fred's Pool Hall watching intently while Moon removed his shoes.

Before Moon could commence his spiel about the virtues of Beautiful Bipeds, the stranger began to speak in a low, comforting voice.

"How would you like to be as rich as Midas?" the stranger asked.

Having no idea who Midas was, Moon asked, "Does he live around here?"

"No, dear boy," the stranger replied, "Midas lived in mythology with the ability to turn everything he touched to gold."

"Ain't no gold around here," Moon responded while continuing to untie the stranger's shoes.

"Oh, yes there is black gold beneath the surface of the land hereabouts, just waiting for some bright fellow to extract it from the ground, and you, my friend, can be in on the ground floor."

"What's black gold?" asked Moon.

"Oil, my friend, 'Texas tea'. And you will be my partner in tapping this giant black river under the Jeter farm."

"How's that?" asked Moon.

"Call me Three Fingered Louie," Moon was told. "I am convinced that there is a large fortune in oil lying beneath the Homer Jeter farm. However, when I presented a lease to Mr. Jeter he threatened me with a sawed off shotgun."

Moon giggled. "Sounds like Uncle Homer," he told Three Fingered Louie.

"But you, my dear Moon, can persuade him to give me a mineral lease on his property. I will pay him $300.00 an acre for the lease and will give him a royalty interest of 1/8th of all oil and gas produced. I will pay all drilling and completion costs. And if you will assist me in obtaining the lease I will pay you an overriding royalty of 1/16th."

"What's drillin' costs?" inquired Moon.

"It is the cost of drilling a hole in the ground just like a water well, but it's much deeper than a water well," Three Fingered Louie told him.

Moon could not comprehend simple figures, let alone percentages. "How much will I get?" Moon inquired.

"If we strike oil you will get enough money to purchase sport cars, vacation homes and accommodating women. The world will be your oyster. Can you imagine spending winters in Florida and summers in Colorado? Flying in jet planes to Paris, London and Rome? Rubbing shoulders with the jet set, Hollywood stars, royalty? It all can be yours, my friend, if you do me this small favor."

Moon was very happy in south Arkansas. None of the promises addressed by Three Fingered Louie appealed to him other than accommodating women. H could always talk with Sweetpea and get his thoughts.

"Let me study about it," Moon told him.

"Excellent," said Three Fingered Louie. "My temporary abode is the Guest Quarters in downtown El Dorado. Please contact me with all due dispatch."

Moon removed his left shoe and placed it in a purple loafer with green tassels. Only $39.95," Moon announced.

"I'll take three pair," Louie told him. And Moon had made a friend for life.

Moon found Sweetpea tinkering over the engine of his souped up Lincoln. He asked Sweetpea, "How'd you like to be rich as Mr. Milds?"

"Mister who?" Sweetpea responded. "The only Milds I know is Jethro Miles, the stable hand at the All Right Corral."

"Naw," said Sweetpea. "This old geezer could touch stuff and turn it to gold."

"Bull shit," said Sweetpea.

Moon could see that this approach was not working. He decided on the direct approach.

"Three Fingered Louie told me oil is the same as gold 'cept it's black."

Sweetpea looked thoughtful. "Could old man Milds turn water to oil?" he asked.

"Nope", Moon, proud in his new found knowledge of the inner works of the oil patch told him. "You just drill a hole in the ground and oil comes out."

"Don't want no hole in our farm," Sweetpea countered.

Moon told him, "He'll pay $300.00"

Sweetpea was perplexed. You mean he'll pay 300 bucks to drill a hole in the ground?" he asked in an astonished voice.

Moon gravely nodded his head.

"Why Moon, I always figgered you was as worthless as a one legged man in an ass kicking contest, but here you done made one smart deal. I'll go tell Daddy Homer about the money and you tell your buddy to bring $300.00 and his spade. He can start diggin' soon as we git the money," Sweetpea told him.

Old Homer was elated when he was paid $300.00 an acre rather than a mere $300.00. He was even more delighted when six months later there were three completed oil wells all pumping over 500 barrels of high grade crude oil each day.

The Homers and Moon all had fat bank accounts. However, other than an increase of visits to Maxine's by Moon, nothing changed. White Lightning still flowed through the still at the Jeter Ranch (now called a ranch rather than a farm). In truth the Jeter property has stayed exactly the same as it always was, barren and desolate except for the three derricks reaching skyward. The house remains unpainted. Moon continues to untie shoes for unwary customers. Nothing really changes in El Dorado.